MY SMOKY BACON CRISP OBSESSION

J. A. BUCKLE

Curious Fox

First published in 2015 by Curious Fox,
an imprint of Capstone Global Library Limited,
7 Pilgrim Street, London, EC4V 6LB
Registered company number: 6695582

www.curious-fox.com

Cover designed by Richard Parker
Cover illustration by Ozerina Anna (Shutterstock)

ISBN 978 1 78202 320 3

19 18 17 16 15
10 9 8 7 6 5 4 3 2 1

A CIP catalogue for this book is available from the British
Library.

Typeset in Palatino & Weiss

Printed and bound by CPI Group (UK) Ltd,
Croydon, CR0 4YY

Huge thanks to Geoff and Lexi.

Tuesday 7th September

9.15am: Sixth form college (English block)

"Some very interesting views of life-changing events," says Mr Parry (or "Andy", as he likes to be called), as he walks round the classroom handing back our essays. "Sophie – great account of the Apollo 11 lunar landings! Amy – awesome effort on the suffragette movement!"

Andy paused. "And Josh... Ah, Josh... Well, I'm not quite sure what to say about your essay. I guess for some people getting the latest Metallica album *might* be thought of as life-changing..."

"Umm," I say. I'm not sure whether Andy is impressed or not. Unfortunately my sarcasm detectors have started whirring. So probably not.

"However, I'm guessing you didn't read the second half of the question," continues Andy. "Life-changing events and *how they have inspired society?*"

"Oh," I say.

The class giggles nervously. This is only our second English lesson at college and everyone is getting to know one another. People are checking out who's cool, who's smart and who's a sad, pathetic loser who can't read questions properly.

4.15pm: Outside college, leant casually against wall

"Yo biatch, wat up?" says Ollie, coming over to give me a fist bump.

For some reason, Ollie now talks like a crystal meth dealer.

"Yo! Yo! Yo! S'all sweet, bro!" I say, but my heart's not really in it.

Ollie tells me about his first Psychology lesson. "Dude," he says. "I found out today dat 'psychology' starts with a P! Thatz some weird shit, ain't it?"

"It's some crazy-ass shit, Ollie," I agree.

Davey comes out of the Art block in jeans and a denim jacket. Very few people can get away with double denim – and Davey isn't one of them.

We start walking home. College is in the town centre and since we are always ravenous, we usually stop off at the supermarket to see what's edible in the Drastically Reduced section. Today I buy some flattened fresh cream éclairs.

"So where's Peter Boy?" mumbles Ollie through mouthfuls of doughnut.

"He's got problems at home," I say. "He texted me to say he was up all night listening to his parents argue."

"Should think himself lucky," says Davey. "I had to listen to mine having rampant..."

"Damn it, Davey!" I say. "You've put me right off my éclair!"

Wednesday 8th September

8.15am: Inner Sanctum, getting ready for college

A problem with college is that you have to wear your own clothes, and I don't have any. At least, I don't have any cool ones. Mum thinks I can wear my school trousers, but if she thinks I'm wearing school uniform to college, she's either very mean or soft in the head. And one thing she isn't is soft in the head. Anyway, I have found some jeans that are only a couple of decades out of fashion, so they'll have to do.

"OK then," I tell Ozzy, lifting him out of his cage. "There's been a slight hiccup with yesterday's embarrassing episode in English, but I think I can still pull it back."

Ozzy does one of his little ferret dances on my lap, showering me with affection and what I hope is only saliva.

"I have managed to get through my first lessons in Chemistry, Maths and Biology without blowing anything up, revealing I'm a complete dickhead, or audibly farting. Yes, there's hope for me yet, Ozzy. It's a brand new start. Who knows, I may even become cool!"

Ozzy gives me a doubtful look.

"Fair enough," I say.

Thursday 9th September

2.30pm: Inner Sanctum

Only two lessons today, so I am home nice and early. Now I'm at college, I've been thinking I could do with some new aims in life, and decide to make a list in my leather-bound notebook.

Yes, I know making lists is incredibly lame but I can't help it – I'm a *making lists* kind of person. Last year, I wrote down five things to achieve and managed to do three of them, which is a 60% success rate, or a grade B. If I can get a B on any of my A levels I'll be well pleased! Anyway, here are my goals for the not too distant future:

1. Make progress with Becky. By which I mean move beyond a one-second kiss on the cheek towards some upper-body-related action. (Lower-body-related action will probably be several years off, unless we're talking foot massage).

2. Make some new college friends and get a band together!

3. Get a Children of Bodom tattoo.

4. Pass at least one of my A levels.

5. Stop making lame lists!!!

Friday 10th September

8.20am: Kitchen, having breakfast

"Where's Mum?" I ask my sister.

"She had to go out," says Maddie.

"What – this early? She doesn't normally start work till ten."

"Well, I don't know!" says Maddie. "I'm not her mother, am I?"

"No," I say. "She's *our* mother."

My sister looks confused for a second. "Right... Er, why

are you eating smoky bacon crisps for breakfast?" she goes on. "That's hardly a balanced diet."

"A balanced diet," I say, "is a bag of crisps in each hand!"

My sister rolls her eyes but doesn't say any more. I allow her a moment to appreciate my excellent comeback before smiling and heading out the door.

9.25am: Chemistry lab

Today, we have to do our first practical. This is worrying because I do not know a single person in my Chemistry set. In some ways this is good (no prior knowledge of my uncoolness!) but then again, I have no idea who I'm going to work with. There's a guy sat beside me who I've nodded at, but he's probably already sussed out a partner; he looks the popular, together type.

"So," says Paula, our teacher, gesturing towards the instructions on the whiteboard. "Today we are going to make ammonia and investigate its solubility. Remember that ammonia is highly pungent and occasionally deadly, so try not to inhale the fumes. Once you have read through all the instructions, please choose a partner and get started."

The guy sat next to me turns my way and smiles.

"You wanna work together?" he says.

Saved!!!

"Hmm, yeah, if you like," I say, shrugging.

The guy turns out to be called Lloyd. He looks a bit like President Obama, only shorter, skinnier and about forty years younger.

"So, how come you're doin' Chemistry?" I say, in an effort to fill the silence.

"I wanna start cooking crack," he says. "I'm gonna be the biggest drug producer this side of Croydon!"

"Really?" I whisper, looking round in case anyone heard.

"No," laughs Lloyd. "I want to be a chemical engineer."

"Oh, right."

"How about you?" he asks. "What d'you wanna do?"

"Well, I'm not sure," I say. "To be honest, I'd like to go into the music business. I play a bit of guitar..."

"Me too," says Lloyd. "Though bass is really my thing."

"Cool," I say. "You into R&B?"

Lloyd shakes his head. "Nope, I'm into metal: deathcore, melodic death and porno-grind mostly."

My eyes mist over and I start to sway a little. Luckily, I can blame it on the fumes of ammonia.

Saturday 11th September

2.00pm: Inner Sanctum

I should really be doing homework but instead I have spent the last four hours working on a design for my tattoo. This is important, though, seeing as it's gonna be on my body for the rest of my life. Not to mention the afterlife, if there is one.

I am not religious but of all religions I think I like reincarnation the best. I'd try and come back as a bonobo ape as they have large brains, muscular bodies and, if David Attenborough is to be believed, a great sex life!

I wonder if people get reincarnated with their tattoos. No, that's silly: you never see animals walking round with tacky slogans, stars or hearts on their legs.

Then again, who knows what's under all that fur?

6.00pm: Inner Sanctum

Finally, after many hours of blood, sweat and tears (well, sweat anyway) I have the perfect design. It includes my favourite pet (Ozzy), my favourite band (Children of Bodom) and the obligatory skull and scythe.

I drift off into a daydream where I'm at an after-gig party. A few attractive girls are leaning on my arms in an adoring kinda way, when one (jet-black hair, large emerald eyes, huge boobs) notices my tattoo. Somewhere, a crappy romantic song starts playing. The girl tosses back her hair in slow motion, gazes tenderly into my eyes and breathes, "Have you got any washing?"

"Huh?"

Over by the door my mum sighs and shakes her head. "Washing, Josh. I'm putting a load on."

Sunday 12th September

10am: Walking to Ned's

I'm on the way to my dad's (AKA Ned's) when I nearly fall over myself trying not to step on a snail. Honestly, I don't know what is up with snails. Do they have a death wish? Anyway, after checking to see no one's looking, I pick it up and place it in some bushes. I wonder what it's thinking now? It would be like someone lifting a person up from Croydon High Street and dumping them in the Brazilian rainforest. It must be like, WTF just happened?

It's a bit naff rescuing kamikaze snails but at least Becky understands. She once had a pet woodlouse!* I haven't heard from Becky for a while so I text her to say hi before knocking on Ned's door.

Me and Ned meet up about twice a week now. I guess I should call him Dad as he *is* my dad, but somehow it's easier to stick with Ned. You'd think after sixteen years of believing someone else was my father, it would feel really weird hanging out with Ned. But it's actually weird how normal it feels.

"Oh, am I glad to see you," Ned says, manoeuvring his wheelchair aside to let me in. "Minty needs her flea treatment."

"Really?" I say, wearily. Minty is a Yorkshire terrier who

---

* *This was in the days before her mum let her graduate to keeping guinea pigs, of course.*

aspires to be a pitbull. If any dog should be controlled under the Dangerous Dogs Act, it's her.

"We'll be OK," says Ned happily. "I'll just get the reinforced gloves."

Monday 13th September

1.45pm: Biology

Even though Davey is to science what badgers are to ballet, he has decided to take Biology because he wants to be a veterinary nurse.

Our teacher (Lorna, who is not unattractive for an education professional) tells us that today we will be dissecting the heart. A few of the girls look worried but me and Davey just grin.

"Bring it on," says Davey.

Lorna starts handing out the hearts on metal trays. I gotta say, the smell isn't great. A few people have their hands over their noses.

"Lightweights," scoffs Davey.

"Pussies," I agree.

"So how's Chemistry going?" says Davey.

"Oh, OK. I made a new mate," I say. "His name's Lloyd."

"Like the bank!" says Davey. "Cool. I haven't made any new friends yet."

"Well, there's plenty of time," I tell him. "And, anyway, why would you want new friends when you know someone as stupendously awesome as me?"

Davey says, "Yeah, right," in a sarcastic WTF way, which is a bit hurtful given that I was only half joking.

"Don't be shy with your heart," says Lorna. "Use your fingers to have a jolly good poke about!"

I pick up the heart carefully. It's covered in yellowy fat and as slippery as a hyperactive ferret in body lotion. I prod around a bit and manage to find four rubbery tubes coming out at the top. Unfortunately, I have a pretty active gag reflex and I suddenly sense the chicken nuggets I had for lunch wanting to make an appearance. I bite my lower lip and keep on prodding while Davey puts coloured clips in to mark the veins.

"Once you've located the main blood vessels," says Lorna, "you'll need to take your scalpel and slice the heart in two to expose the chambers. You may want to remove some of the fatty tissue first."

I bite my lip even harder and start to carve away some of the fat. Urgh. This is disgusting. Especially the smell.

"I like to call this the McDonald's Cut," Lorna goes on cheerfully as she wanders round the room. "Once sliced, you'll see that the heart resembles the sort of bun people use for yummy double cheeseburgers!"

"Er, I'm feeling a bit weird, Davey," I say, dropping the scalpel and sitting down hard. "Can you take over for a bit?"

Davey looks at me like an electrocuted owl, before crashing to the ground in a heap.

Tuesday 14th September

7.15pm: Inner Sanctum with Davey, Peter, Ollie and Ozzy

"That's it, then," says Davey. "I have to apply to a new college.

There's a good one in Epsom. It's only twenty miles away. Or I could travel down to Crawley; they've got a railway station."

Davey, Peter and Ollie are slumped on my bed like comatose slugs. It's no wonder my mattress has lost all its puffiness.

"Don't be silly," I tell Davey. "It wasn't that bad."

"You said people were screaming!"

"That's because you pulled the tray down on top of you. There was rancid fat and bits of heart flying everywhere. It was like a scene from a slasher movie."

"Well," says Peter. "What can they expect, taking a horrible subject like Biology? I can assure you, you don't get showered in body parts in Textiles and Graphic Design."

"Exactly," I say. "And that girl who vommed? Well, her face was green well before you fainted."

Davey sighs. "Fine. I guess I'll be OK if we don't have to dissect anything else. There aren't any other dissections, are there?"

"Nah," I say. I decide not to mention the pig's eyeball coming up in the fourth module.

"So you goin' out with anyone yet?" I ask Ollie, in order to change the subject.

"Working on it, bro. Let's just say there's possibilities."

I nod, impressed. Over in his cage, Ozzy does his impersonation of a surprised meerkat, which means he thinks Ollie is lying.

"What about you and Becky?" says Peter.

"Oh, it's OK," I say. "We're OK."

"You seen her boobs?" says Ollie.

"Of course," I say. "But, er, only through clothing."

"Dude, *everyone's* seen 'em through clothing!" laughs Ollie. "You 'ad a feel?"

"I have had a brief fondle, as it happens."

"Wow!" says Davey, his glasses fogging up.

"Actually," I say, "fondle is not really the word but there was... contact."

"Contact?" asks Ollie.

"I had to push past her in the Science corridor. It was busy and there were all these people so we had to squash up..."

"Hmm," says Peter. "*How long* have you been going out?"

"I know," I say, "but Becky is embarrassed about her boobs. She feels they are all people see when they look at her."

"She's right," says Ollie.

"We get on OK, though. I mean... not in a sexual sense but talking – we do a lot of talking. Or at least Becky does. About her boobs. And how much she hates them. But still..."

"You're communicating," agrees Peter. "That's more than my folks are doing."

Everyone is quiet while Peter picks a few stray ferret hairs off his trousers.

"I don't think they get on that well any more," he says finally.

"What makes you say that?" says Davey.

"My mum calls my dad a lazy, self-centred bastard. And my dad calls my mum a cow."

10.00pm: Inner Sanctum

I feel bad for Peter, so I take out my leather-bound notebook and begin to write a song for him, but it feels kinda creepy so I write one for Becky instead.

My body feels so alien

These breasts, they are no fun

I wish I could be 34B

And not bounce when I run.

From the album: *Alien Breasts* by Josh Walker

Hmm, on second thoughts, I don't think I'll give this to Becky. She may take it the wrong way. Girls can be weird like that.

Wednesday 15th September

6.00pm: Kitchen

"It's me making tea tonight," says my sister, waving a saucepan dangerously. "Beans on toast."

"Oh, please, not that!" I say. "Becky's coming over later and I wanna blow her away with my awesomeness, not my farts."

"Yeah, well, good luck with that," says my sister.

"Why can't we wait for Mum to do something when she gets in?" I say.

"I don't want to bother Mum," says my sister. "She'll be tired from doing her cleaning all day. Now hush up and get some plates out."

7.12pm

Becky was supposed to be here at 7. Maybe she isn't coming. Or maybe my clock is fast. I think it is a little fast, maybe...

7.15pm

My clock isn't fast! I've just checked on the internet and if anything it's slow! Right, so, obviously she isn't coming. Great! Nice work, Becky. Thanks a lot!

7.20pm

Oh well, at least my farts have eased off a bit. It's important to look on the bright side.

7.25pm

She doesn't like me any more! She's got someone else who's cooler and better-looking. Well, fine. No problem. I hope he likes you as much as I did, Becky. You obviously don't appreciate a good thing when you see it...

7.26pm

Yes!! The doorbell!

7.27pm: Inner Sanctum

"Sorry I'm late," says Becky, following me into the room.

"Oh, are you?" I say. "I hadn't noticed."

Becky sits beside me on the bed and stares into my face.

"Josh," Becky says, "I need you to do something for me."

"Um, OK," I say.

"I want you to close your eyes."

"Huh?" I say.

"Close your eyes."

I do as I'm told and listen to some rustling and a few grunts.

"OK," she says. "You can open them now."

"Jesus!" I say blinking. "Becky, you're in your bra!" I'm not sure what to think about this. I should be really excited but, to be honest, it's a bit unexpected. I'm not used to seeing people in their bras (unless they're in the Next catalogue).

"I want you to tell me honestly," says Becky. "Are they too big?"

"Are what too big?" I say, stalling for time.

Becky raises her eyebrows. "Just tell me honestly!" she says.

"You *really* want me to be honest?" I say.

"I *really* do," she says.

"In that case," I say, "no, they aren't. The thing you gotta understand, Becky, is that the words *too big* and *boobs* do not really belong in the same sentence."

Becky sighs and replaces her sweatshirt. "I'm disappointed in you, Josh," she says. "I thought you were different from the others. I thought you liked me for more than one thing."

"Two things," I say. "Er, no, wait. Sorry, Becky, I'm joking. It was a joke!"

"Right, well, I'm outta here," says Becky, getting up in a huff.

"Becks," I say. "Wait. I was wrong... they *are* too big. I dunno how you cope with such humongous boobs. It must be a total nightmare..."

But Becky and her boobs have gone.

Thursday 16th September

4.35pm: Inner Sanctum

Quite a good day at college today.

Firstly, I got an A on my Maths homework. Maths is definitely my best subject. I got 85 out of 100 questions right, which is well over 90%.

Secondly, I managed to answer a question correct in Chemistry, my worst subject.

And thirdly, I found out that Lloyd likes Children of Bodom, my favourite band! He has all their albums and a Children of Bodom patch on his jacket. He hasn't seen them in the tattooed flesh, though, unlike yours truly.

Talking of tattoos, I've found a good place locally that seems OK. At least, I couldn't hear any screaming when I walked past yesterday. I plan to check them out on Saturday.

7.15pm: Scouts

I am now way too old for Scouts but Mum says I still have to go and be a young leader (general dogsbody), as it'll look good in job interviews. To be honest, I don't mind. There's the occasional toasted marshmallow and it's a chance to catch up with Peter, who I don't see much at college, what with him doing all the trendy (dossy) subjects.

Today, our leader Sean's been a lazy bastard and not organised anything, so we're playing "bored" games.

I'm in charge of Monopoly which is worrying because:

1. It contains small parts and some of the Scouts in my group have the mental age of toddlers.

2. It can go on for ten hours.

3. I hate it.

Typically, that jammy git Peter got Mouse Trap, though the elastic band will probably be missing.

Anyway, my group of four sit down at one of the tables and, needless to say, there's an argument straight off about who is going to have what counter. In the end I have to pull rank and threaten not to play if I can't be the Scottie dog.

After about thirty seconds, it is clear this is going to be a two-horse race between me and Wentworth. Wentworth is thirteen and so one of the older Scouts, although he's so short and baby-faced he looks about seven (months). Billy (ten) has gone off to watch Mouse Trap (Sean found a substitute elastic band) and Alex (also ten) is throwing the Monopoly money up in the air, laughing hysterically and yelling, "I'm rich. RICH!!"

Wentworth chucks the dice, sending it flying across the board. "Six!" he cries. He smacks his boot counter down. "Four, five, six... Ha! Community Chest. Collect £10 from each player. Come on, losers, hand it over!"

Wentworth is obviously going all out to win. People like him really annoy me. It's supposed to be a bit of fun, FFS! Anyway, with a pathetic self-centred attitude like that I will have to beat him at any cost.

I hand him the tenners from myself and the other two players, who are now nowhere to be seen. I probably should go and find them. They might be on a train halfway to Edinburgh by now.

"Come on, bumface," snarls Wentworth.

I throw the dice and get a three.

"Ha! Go to jail, loser," says Wentworth.

9.05pm

"Well," I say. "It's time to go home. Let's call it a draw."

"Nope, let's call me the winner!" says Wentworth, grinning.

"Fine," I say. "Well done!"

It's annoying, letting him win, but everyone else is leaving and I don't want to spend any longer with Wentworth than is absolutely necessary.

"Er, we could carry on playing at my house?" says Wentworth. "Then we'd really find out who the winner is."

WTF?

"I only live round the corner, 24 Wilton Avenue," he goes on. "We'd be there in five minutes."

"Um, no, that's OK," I say. "You've got more money than me so it's only fair that you're the winner."

Wentworth shrugs and walks away, leaving me to pack up the game. Play at his house? I'd rather superglue my pubes to a speeding vehicle.

Friday 17th September

6.30pm: Returning from trip to Tesco with Ned and Minty, the Yorkshire Terror

Ned's wheelchair is so laden down with shopping that all I can see of Minty is the tips of her ears. Hopefully she isn't suffocating beneath all the Buy-One-Get-One-Free toilet rolls. Of course, if I had a car, like *most* people my age, transporting small dogs would not be a problem. I must remember to mention that to Mum as yet another excellent excuse, I mean *reason*, for me getting a car.

Ned's house is about ten minutes further on from ours and my arms are getting tired.

"You know, you should ask Mum if you can move in with us," I say. "Then you could sell your house and get some money for things like holidays and, er, cars."

"Your mum wants her own space," says Ned.

"Well, that's just silly," I say.

Ned says, "You can get a bird to land on your head, Josh, but you can't make it build a nest."

Ned occasionally comes out with stuff like this on the way back from Tesco.

Sometimes I don't have a clue what he's on about. Actually, I *never* have a clue what he's on about, but I do know that Mum is dead against the two of them sharing a home. When I asked her about it she said, "I like Ned very much, Josh, but he collects beer mats," as if beer mats were like shrunken heads or something.

Saturday 18th September

10.30am: Tattoos 'R' Us waiting room

Tattoos 'R' Us seem to specialise in designs of the naked women variety. I have probably learnt more about women's anatomy from these waiting room walls than all my Biology lessons put together.

The waiting room is small, dark and slightly intimidating. If hell had a waiting room, it'd probably look like this. Also, I'm a bit scared.* People on *Yahoo Answers* said the pain varied from a mild bee sting to a near-death experience. Looking around, this is the sort of place I can imagine having a near-death experience.

And when I say "a bit scared" I mean bloody terrified!

A guy appears from behind a red velvet curtain, says "hi" and gives me a big smile. He looks familiar and then I realise he is the spitting image of a highly tattooed Freddy Krueger from *A Nightmare on Elm Street* – including the hat and filed-down teeth.

I say, "Yo," and give him the paper with my drawing on.

"Nice work," he lisps. "It'll cost around £80."

"No sweat," I say. "I got the dough, yo." I seem to have adopted Ollie's meth-dealer talk in my nervousness.

Freddy grins. "That's good," he says. "What's your date of birth?"

"July 4th," I say.

"What year?"

"Every year?"

Freddie raises a heavily pierced eyebrow. "I'm gonna have to see ID."

"Oh yo, sure," I say, patting my pockets pointedly. "Except I think I may have, um, left it at home..."

"Sorry," he says. "No tattoos 'til you're eighteen. It's the law."

He gives me a pointy grin and flicks a long-taloned finger towards the door. "See you in a few years. Yo!"

11.45am: Inner Sanctum

A few years! I cannot believe Freddie thought I was fifteen. It's an insult to my obvious sophistication and maturity.

Oh well. I cross out aim number three in my leather-bound notebook and go downstairs to get some crisps and a *Bob the Builder* ice lolly to cheer myself up.

Sunday 19th September – Ozzy's 7th birthday

10.00am: Inner Sanctum

Today is Ozzy's birthday. Actually, today is the anniversary of when I got him as a kit, so today definitely *isn't* his birthday. It was probably a few weeks ago, which means I've missed it. Damn.

Anyway, Ozzy has some nice presents. Becky, who has forgiven me for getting the answer about her boobs wrong, gave me a stuffed vole at college (artificial, thankfully). Peter came round with some air freshener, which I assume is more for me than Ozzy, since Ozzy doesn't give a rat's ass about stinking the place out. Ollie gave him a small pack of plastic balls with metal bells in and Davey gave him a packet of chicken crunchies which, take it from me, smell a helluva lot nicer than they taste!

Mum leans against the doorframe and watches Ozzy playing with Ollie's balls – the plastic ones, not Ollie's actual testicles.

"He's still got plenty of life in him, hasn't he," she says.

"'Course, Mum," I say. "He's only seven."

"That's not a bad age for a ferret, Josh," says Mum. "They don't live forever, you know. None of us do."

"Shush, Mum," I say. "He'll hear you!"

She smiles a little and comes over to ruffle my hair before leaving. Damn, I must've told Mum a million times that the hair is not to be ruffled! Now that my hair is longer (brushing top of shoulders) it has a slight tendency towards frizz, and I need to keep it sleeked down.

Oh well, Ozzy seems happy enough despite Mum's little speech. I could watch him play all day but unfortunately I've got a Chemistry test tomorrow so I'd better start revising.

Monday 20th September

4.00pm: Chemistry

"Time's up," says Paula. "Please put down your pens."

I feel a bit shell-shocked and it must show because Lloyd asks me if I'm OK.

"I'm fine," I lie. "That was a piece of piss."

"I found it quite difficult," says Lloyd, looking worried.

"Yeah, well," I say. "When I say piece of piss, I mean... I mean a piece of piss for someone who's got a bladder infection that actually makes it quite hard for them to piss."

"Ah... um... right," says Lloyd.

I've been wondering for a while whether to ask Lloyd if he's in a band. If not, he might be up for starting one with me, seeing as we're into the same stuff and that. It's kinda embarrassing asking, a bit like asking a girl out on a date, but it would be great to be able to tick off number two from my list!

"So, um, Lloyd," I say. "I guess with you being into music and playing bass an' all, you're probably in a band?"

"Yeah," says Lloyd.

"Oh, right," I say. "Sure, yeah. I knew that..."

Oh well, I'm not that bothered. There'll be other people to ask.

8.00pm

I'm extremely bothered, and there aren't.

Tuesday 21st September

3.05pm: Eldritch Portal (front door)

"Oh," says Mum, looking surprised and slightly annoyed to see me as she comes out of the house. "Why are you here?"

"I live here, Mum. I'm your son, remember?"

"But I thought you'd be back about half past four."

"Maths was cancelled," I say. "The teacher said we were all beyond hope and not worth teaching."

"Oh, right," she says, rooting through her bag.

"More to the point," I say, "why are *you* here? Aren't you supposed to be at work?"

Mum zips up her bag. "I, er, just popped back to, um, get something. That's all, love. Nothing for you to worry about."

"Um, OK," I say. "Will you be back in time to do tea?"

Mum checks her watch. "Should be. Should be. Got to dash, love. Bye."

Cool! With Mum out of the way I can turn my amp up full volume!

Wednesday 22nd September

12.50pm: Lunch in college canteen with Peter, Davey and Ollie

Peter sighs and starts eating his second banana. "If things get much worse at home," he says, "I may have to eat three of these in a row."

"Sorry?" I say.

"If you eat three bananas in a row you die," says Peter.

"Bullshit," says Ollie.

"It's true," says Peter. "It's the potassium levels."

I give Peter a friendly thump on the back while sneakily taking a look in his bag to see if there are any more bananas in there. There aren't, but there is something a bit odd. It's a book about witchcraft. Maybe it's something to do with one of his 'trendy' courses. Let's hope so.

"Parents," I say to Peter, shaking my head.

"They's bitches," says Ollie.

"Mine are quite nice, actually," says Davey.

2.45pm: Becky's house

I haven't seen or heard from Becky for a few days, so I go round for a surprise visit. She invites me in and we talk for a while, but then she says has to clean out her guinea pigs' cages. I offer to help, as I am an expert on the care of small mammals, but apparently they are nervous of strangers. There's been no opportunity for any upper-body-related action. Not even a kiss.

Thursday 23rd September

7.15pm: Hallway

Mum looks me up and down. "Very smart," she says.

"Do I *have* to go to Scouts?" I ask.

"It'll be good for your CV," says Mum.

"Not if I kill one of them," I say.

7.35pm: Scouts

Awesome! Who do I have in my group again but Wentworth? And

as if that wasn't bad enough, today we are making penholders from toilet rolls!

"I don't want to do this. It's lame," says Wentworth.

I agree, but the last time I said something was lame in Scouts, Sean got really animated with me. And not in a good way.

"Well, we have to do it," I say, grabbing a pile of old gift wrap, tissue paper and tangled wool. "Look, we've got some nice materials here. Choose something you like and your holder could look really professional."

"Yeah, right," says Wentworth.

I decide to make my penholder for Becky. Her favourite colours are black and dark purple but there isn't any paper in those colours, so she'll have to make do with yellow and fluorescent pink.

"This is gay," says Wentworth.

"It's fine," I say.

"Yeah, well, you would say that 'cause you're gay too."

I put my hands on my hips and give Wentworth what I hope is a 'don't screw with me' look.

"See?" says Wentworth.

Sighing loudly, I start wrapping the paper around my holder. "I'm not gay, Wentworth," I go on. "Why would you say that?"

"You act gay."

"Er, no, I don't."

"Er, *yes*, you do."

"Er, *NO!* I DON'T!"

"ER, *YES you do! AND NO RETURN!*"

Damn!

"Look," I say, "this is getting us nowhere. *How* do I act gay, exactly?"

"You've got girly hair, you go around with that gay guy Peter, you've got an earring in the gay ear and you chose *fluorescent pink* tissue paper!"

Hmm. I realise, with a sinking feeling, that everything Wentworth has just said is annoyingly spot on...

"Yeah, well, all of that may be annoyingly spot on," I say, "but here's the thing, Wentworth: *I've* got a girlfriend and if I was gay I'd have a *boyfriend*, wouldn't I?"

"I know," says Wentworth. "You're going out with Becky. She's friends with my sister."

"Oh," I say. "Well..."

"She's a lezzer!"

"Now, hold on..."

"What's going on here?" says Peter, wandering over. "Oh, I like that pink, Josh."

"He's gay and his so-called *girlfriend's* a lezzer," says Wentworth, jabbing a finger at me.

"I think you're getting confused," says Peter, smiling. "I'm actually the gay one. Josh's relationship with me is purely platonic."

Wentworth's eyes widen.

"It means *non*-sexual," I say hurriedly.

"Whatever," says Wentworth. "Becky's still a big fat lezzer!"

Peter sighs. "Just ignore him, Josh."

"A big fat lezzer with ginormous tits!"

Oh. My. God. I am suddenly furious. So furious that I grab Wentworth's penholder and crush it in one hand, like a bodybuilder crushing a can.

"Hey, that's my thingy!" cries Wentworth, looking round in all directions. "Sean! Josh busted my penholder! I worked hard on that! SEAN!"

"I'll bust *you* in a minute," I growl. "How dare you slag off Becky and her boobs when she's not here to defend herself? You are the sort of person who goes to a lake and throws stones for the ducks instead of bread; who presses the button on crossings when you don't even *need to cross!*"

"Bit harsh," says Peter.

"I don't care," I say. "It's true. He's the Spawn of the Devil!"

"Er, Josh," says Peter.

I look down at my feet. "Sean's behind me, isn't he?"

10.10pm: Inner Sanctum

I have a three-week suspension from Scouts, which is pretty infuriating as next week they are going abseiling and the week after that, go-karting. Well, anyway, I hope Wentworth forgets to do up his safety harness and breaks his neck. I can just imagine his wimpy little body tumbling down the side of a sheer cliff, his head smacking into the sharp, jagged rocks, his limbs twisting in horrible... Er, I probably need to stop this.

10.15pm

Thing is, though, if it's true what he said about Becky being a lesbian, then how will I ever get any upper-body-related action?

Friday 24th September

11.00am: Maths with Ollie

Ollie informs me that he is taking driving lessons and that his parents are buying him a ten-year-old Ford Escort in dark metallic gold.

"We can cruise the streets in my pimp mobile," says Ollie. "We'll be like kings. Or I'll be king as I'm the driver, but you'll be like my chief advisors or somethin'."

I'd love to share Ollie's enthusiasm but I don't think lurching up and down the high street in the passenger seat of an elderly sparkly brown Ford Escort is likely to inspire much awe.

Or it could just be that I'm jealous, of course.

3.10pm: Chemistry

Paula hands me back my test paper without saying anything.

She's given it a J.

"I've got a J," I tell Lloyd.

"Er, I think that's a U," says Lloyd.

"A U?" I say, looking back at the paper.

"It's not that bad," says Lloyd (who got a C, the flash bastard).

"It's very bad," I say, sighing.

"Yes, it is," says Lloyd. "But look on the bright side, you can only get better!"

"Damn," I say. "My life sucks at the moment. Everyone is getting cars and playing in bands and being with girlfriends who are happy to engage in upper-body-related action."

"*I* don't have a girlfriend," says Lloyd, "or a car."

"But you're in a band!" I say accusingly.

Lloyd folds his test paper and puts it in the back of his Chemistry book. "About that," he says. "It's... well, it's a church band."

"A church band?"

"We have two women in their sixties who sing and play tambourines, my dad on accordion and, on very bad days, my eight-year-old cousin on maracas."

"Ah," I say, accidentally grinning. "Not exactly metal, then?"

"Not exactly."

I don't want to be mean, especially as Lloyd looks a bit crushed, but hell, yeah, this is brilliant!

We push in our chairs and start filing out of the classroom. "So," I say, trying to play it cool, "does this band take up all your spare time, or would you maybe wanna come round to mine sometime and do a bit of jammin'? I mean, we could, you know, think about startin' our *own* band. A proper metal one with serious death and porno-grind influences?"

"I thought you'd never ask!" says Lloyd.

Saturday 25th September

3.30pm: Returning from Tesco with Ned and Minty in wheelchair

"There's this kid at Scouts," I say to Ned, "who's really got it in for me. We had an argument. I accidentally called him Spawn of the Devil and now I'm banned."

Ned nods gravely.

"He's a right dick," I say.

"Hmm," says Ned, while opening a bag of smoky

bacon crisps. (Why he can't eat the salt and vinegar ones we've got, I don't know.)

"He always acts like a real suck-up with Sean, our leader," I say, as we wait for the green man on the crossing. "And he's really small and baby-faced so I think people think he's cute or something."

"Don't worry," says Ned. "A whitewashed crow will show his black eventually."

WTF?

Sunday 26th September

3.15pm: Inner Sanctum

"Cool ferret," says Lloyd, propping his bass up against the bed and looking in Ozzy's cage.

"Thanks," I say. "His name's Ozzy."

Lloyd puts one hand on his stomach and bows low. "All hail his Royal Ozzness," he says solemnly.

"Dook dook," says Ozzy.

We plug in our amps, tune up and start by playing a few riffs of "Crazy Train" by Ozzy's namesake. I have to admit Lloyd holds down a pretty solid rhythm, but thankfully he's *not quite* as accomplished as me, speed-wise. He doesn't say so, but I can tell he is well impressed by my blisteringly fast and astonishingly accurate solo.

The door creaks open and round pops my sister's heavily made-up face. She isn't going out today, so I don't know why she's put on false eyelashes.

"Well, hi there," she says. "And what's *your* name?"

"Oh hi, I'm Lloyd," says Lloyd.

"Ooh, nice name!" exclaims my sister. "Like the bank."

"Almost," says Lloyd. "Except that the bank's name has an *s* on the end: *Lloydsss*."

"Of course. Silly me," says my sister.

"Not at all," says Lloyd, smiling. "You were almost right."

Then my sister seems to get something in her eyes and starts opening and shutting them wildly.

"Well," I say after watching my sister do this for what seems like hours. "Perhaps me and Lloyd had better get on. Close the door on your way out, Maddie."

Maddie smiles, tosses back her hair and says, "See ya around, Lloyd," in a weird, husky, breathless kinda way.

Lloyd blinks a few times and swallows loudly.

8.45pm: Lounge, half watching TV with Maddie and Mum

"So, you've made a new friend," says Maddie.

"Might've," I say.

"You know what they say about black men, don't you?" she says.

"Now, now," says my mum.

Maddie grins. "As in the size of their..."

"Excuse me," I say. "Number one, Lloyd is *half* black. Number two, that is a very racist and sexist thing to say. And, number three, he is way, and I mean *way*, too young for you!"

"We'll see," says Maddie, leaning back in the sofa and crossing her legs.

I must warn Lloyd. My sister is an out-of-control sexual predator.

Monday 27th September

10.00am: Maths

Why is Becky not an out-of-control sexual predator?

Tuesday 28th September

5.30pm: Inner Sanctum

I am practising sweep picking with the brilliant 'Bed of Razorz' by Children of Bodom (surely one of the most awesome metal riffs of all time) when I receive a text from Becky. It says:

Can I come over. I've got something to show you ;) ;)

I read this again with particular reference to the ending:

something to show you ;) ;)

Well, let's face it, this could be anything. It could be a new handbag. It could be a freakishly long French fry or a tomato in the shape of a rabbit. It could be...

Well, it could be anything!

Except that there's a couple of winks which suggest it's something a bit, well, a bit, er...

I'm about to text back 'What is it?' when Becky texts again:

Coming now. Remember this is for your eyes only.

All right!

5.45pm

I run down the hall but realise I'm looking ridiculously eager, so make myself take baby steps before opening the door.

"Oh, hi," I say casually.

Becky has a real glint in her eye. "I couldn't wait any longer," she says, bouncing up and down like a wallaby on a trampoline. "I got so excited!"

Mum comes out of the kitchen and stands in the hall. "Oh, hi there, Becky, love. How's college going?" she says, shoving me aside slightly.

"Oh, it's OK, thanks," says Becky.

"What subjects are you doing again?"

"History, Geog..."

"Mum," I say, grabbing Becky's arm. "It's the evening, talk about college is banned. Come on, Becky, let's go."

We go into my Inner Sanctum and Becky joins me on the bed and gives me a big kiss on the lips. Oh yes. In your face, Wentworth!

"Thank you so much for being my boyfriend," she says. "I don't know what I'd do without you." She runs her hand through my hair, which would be nice except it's frizzing like mad and a bit tangly.

"I find the crazy, tousled look very sexy," she goes on. "You're cute, Josh... do you know that?"

"Oh, I'm not!" I say, waving her away. "Or maybe just a bit. People have mentioned my eyes. And, er, nose."

"Well, before we get started, I'd better shut the door," she says.

"Right," I say. Now we're talking (or hopefully doing more than talking!).

"Don't want anyone seeing," goes on Becky.

"Nooo," I say.

Becky takes off her sweatshirt and I am thinking, 'OK, this is it, Josh. Keep calm and don't do anything stupid!' But just when

I am wondering whether or not to take off my own sweatshirt (and cursing the fact that I forgot to change my washed-out, baggy *Finding Nemo* vest), she suddenly reaches down into her bag and pulls out a load of leaflets and computer printouts.

"This is what I wanted to show you," she says smiling. "Now, try not to get excited by the pictures. I know you're a boy and they're boobs and all that, but I need your serious and unbiased opinion."

"Um," I say. "What?"

Becky shoves the paperwork in my lap. "What d'you think?"

It turns out that what Becky has to show me is a load of before-and-after breast surgery pictures.

"Do you think I should go for this size or these slightly larger ones?" she asks, now pointing to a couple of pictures. "I think these may be a bit too small, don't you think? What I don't want is to have too much taken off in one go. I think it would be better to do it in stages."

We spend the next thirty minutes poring over the brochures and printouts. I am now an expert on all aspects of breast reduction, including the placing, length and location of incisions, healing times, side effects (potentially horrible) and low-interest payment plans.

"So what do you think?" she says, collecting up the sheets.

I consider for a while, rubbing the bridge of my nose. "I think it's a shame you feel you need to have surgery," I say, "but if they make you really unhappy, then I guess I understand. It's no good going through life being miserable."

Becky gives me a hug and says she has to go.

"Promise me you'll talk it through with your mum first,

though," I say.

"I promise," says Becky.

FML.

Wednesday 29th September

4.30pm: Supermarket – Drastically Reduced section with Ollie, Davey and Peter

The Drastically Reduced section is not looking promising today. There are a couple of bags of slimy pre-prepared salad that would probably be fatal if eaten and some anti-limescale toilet cleaner, which wouldn't do you much good either.

Ollie says, "Yo, homies, how you bustin fo' cheese?"

"The cheese is in aisle four," says Davey.

Ollie rolls his eyes. "I mean, how much money you carryin'?"

I notice a few women casting worried glances at Ollie before clasping their bags to their chests and scurrying away.

"Ollie," I say. "We are not your homies. Oh, and 53p."

"14p," says Peter, the big spender.

"£1.12," says Davey.

"Yo!" says Ollie. "We can loot one of dem big-ass trays of doughnuts, you feel me? The ones with the different coloured icing and shit."

We can't afford a tray, but we do get a pack of four jam-filled ones. Surprisingly, Davey says he'll eat his later.

"Wassup, Davey?" I ask, when we get outside the shop and start walking home.

"I have to do a presentation for my tutor group tomorrow and I feel a bit sick. I'm worried I'll have a panic attack," says Davey.

"Ha," I say.

"No, seriously," says Davey. "It's awful. I come over all hot, like I'm gonna faint. I feel sick and my heart starts beating really, really fast."

"Jesus, Davey," says Peter. "That sounds bad."

Davey digs into the bag of doughnuts anyway. "It is. It's horrible."

"What you oughta do," says Ollie, "is get a pet, ya dig? Like my Bongo. Dogs is great for sortin' stress and shit. I read that someplace."

I can't actually imagine Ollie ever being stressed. Then again, maybe that's because he has a dog.

But Davey isn't convinced. "I can't exactly take a Labrador Retriever to my presentation, can I?"

"You could," says Ollie, "if you was blind."

"But I'm not blind," says Davey.

"Pretend you is," says Ollie simply.

"Or what about a hamster?" suggests Peter.

"Pretend I'm a hamster?"

"Take one in! No one would notice it. You could put it in your pencil case and give it a vigorous stroke whenever you feel your blood pressure rising."

"Hmm," I say. "Number one, keeping a hamster in a pencil case is almost certainly animal abuse..."

"And number two," says Ollie. "Yo pencils would be gnawed ta bits."

"Yes, and number three!!" I say, getting into this. "It'll probably rip yo' finger off!!!"

"I'll just have to take deep breaths, like I always do," says Davey.

8.10pm: Inner Sanctum

I feel bad for Davey and his anxiety problems, so I decide to write him a song. This will hopefully make Davey feel better. Plus, it'll be useful to raise people's awareness of the issues when my band becomes famous.

Blood pulsing

Heart convulsing

Sweat pours down my back

Eyes crying

Feel like dying

Panic. Panic Attack!

(Chorus)

Panic Panic

Panic Panic

It's a panic

A panic attack

Panic Panic

Panic Panic

It's a panic

Yes, a panic attack!!

From the album: *Panic Attacks and Other Anxiety-Related Disorders* by Josh Walker

Thursday 30th September

5.30pm: Inner Sanctum

In English today, we were told to write an essay for homework about something important to us. I immediately thought about Ozzy but Andy says it would make it more interesting, and stretch us more creatively, if we wrote about an inanimate object or place. Maybe I should write about my guitar.

No Scouts today, as I am still banned. This either makes me really hard-ass or really sad. Unfortunately, I think I know which.

Friday 1st October

9.30am: Chemistry

"Wanna do some more jammin' soon?" asks Lloyd.

"Sure," I say. "Maybe I could come round yours?"

"Maybe," he says. "Although it'd be nice to see Ozzy again and, your, um, sister..."

OK, I'm gonna have to stop this right now.

"Lloyd," I say. "I really want you to come round but, although my sister may *seem* nice, she's actually an out-of-control sexual predator."

Lloyd punches the air and cries, "Yes!"

Saturday 2nd October

1.45pm: Davey's house

I have been a bit of a shit friend as I forgot to text Davey to find out how his panic attack went, so I have decided to go round his house.

"I brought this for you, Davey," I say, handing over a piece of paper as he opens his door.

"Oh, wow," says Davey. "You wrote me a song?"

"Er, well, yes. I mean, obviously it's not like a love song or anything. Ha ha!"

"Ha ha!!" says Davey.

"That would be embarrassing," I say.

"*Really* embarrassing," says Davey.

"It's more to help you feel better about your anxiety," I say.

Davey lets me in, closes the door and starts reading. "Well, um, thanks Josh," he says when he gets to the end. "I'm sure... I'm sure that will probably, almost certainly, help, um... a bit..."

"No problem," I say.

"Right."

"So did you have a panic attack during your presentation?" I ask.

"No," says Davey, smiling. "I actually didn't feel too bad. I thought about Ollie's Labrador Bongo just before I did the presentation and it seemed to calm me."

Hmm. I spend ages writing a song while all Ollie has to do is mention his dopey dog.

Sunday 3rd October

3.45pm: Lounge

I text Becky to ask if she's spoken to her mum about the surgery yet. Becky texts back to say not yet. She's building up to it.

I start to text:

Do you fancy coming over?

And then, because I'm thinking I should be a bit more upfront with my feelings, I change it to:

Do you fancy coming over later, you awesome, gorgeous girl?

3.50pm: Lounge

At long last I get a text back from Becky:

Soz, have to clean out my guinea pigs' cages.

Monday 4th October

1.45pm: Biology

Today we are doing an experiment with the water flea Daphnia. We have to put them on a slide and count their heartbeats because, weirdly, they have see-through bodies! Imagine if we had see-through bodies: you could see everything we ate. In my case, a load of mushed-up smoky bacon crisps. Anyway, we have to see how their heartbeats go up when we add caffeine solution.

"Seems a bit cruel," says Davey, getting the pipette ready. "What if it doesn't like coffee?"

"It'll be OK," I say, "Drop it on."

"I didn't expect Biology to turn me into a torturer," says Davey, squeezing on the warm caffeine solution. "Look, his heart's beating really fast now. Oh my God, he's gonna croak!"

Davey starts breathing fast in sympathy with the water flea. Meanwhile, I am trying to count the number of heartbeats but it's difficult with Davey huffing and puffing in my ears.

"A hundred and fifty-two, Davey," I say. "Write it down."

"How's everything going here?" says Lorna.

"Good," I say.

"Are you OK, David?" she says, peering in Davey's face.

"I'm fine," mumbles Davey.

"He's upset about the water flea," I say.

"Oh, don't worry about that," says Lorna cheerfully. "We put them back in the tank just as soon as the experiment is over. They'll be fine."

"I wasn't upset," hisses Davey when Lorna's gone. "Now she thinks I'm a right wuss."

"No, she doesn't," I say. Although I'm pretty sure she does.

Davey sighs. "This anxiety thing is a pain," he says.

"I thought you were OK now," I say.

Davey stares at me like I've just asked him for a snog. "No, Josh, it doesn't go away just like that."

So my song may be useful after all...

"Do you know," says Davey, gently placing a new victim on a clean slide, "when I talk to adults, I can't look them in the eye?"

"Huh?" I say.

"I look them in the teeth," says Davey. "If there was a massive explosion at college, and all my teachers were burnt to ashes, I could help the police identify their remains by their dental records."

"Wow!" I say. "That's a useful skill to have!"

"Not really," says Davey.

Tuesday 5th October

8.35am: Hallway, getting ready to go to college

"Where are my trainers?" I ask Mum.

"In the bin," says Mum.

"What?"

"They were a disgrace, Josh. They stank to high heaven."

I rush to the bin and find my trainers at the very bottom, covered in egg shell and used tea bags.

"A few sprays of Febreeze and they'll be fine," I say.

"Put those filthy things down and wear some other shoes!" yells Mum.

5.45pm: Inner Sanctum

Doing English homework: farewell to old friends

Today I said farewell to my trainers. They had been my companions for over five years. Like a faithful dog, they were always up for a walk: if I had to go somewhere scary, like the tattoo parlour, my trainers always came along for support.

I've put my trainers through a lot. Many's the time I made them walk through dog mess, or worse. Of course, they never complained. Trainers

> are life's troopers.

> But now they are gone. My mother does not understand the bond between a boy and his trainers. Unlike my trainers, she has no soul!

I have just re-read this and am worried it could come across as odd or, worse still, mentally unstable. I can't risk being made to look a borderline-bonkers, attention-seeking idiot twice in one month.

Wednesday 6th October

5.30pm: Inner Sanctum

I am about to blow the roof off this shithole with my guitar when Maddie invites herself in and throws herself on my bed.

"What's this?" she asks, picking up one of the leaflets Becky left on my bedside table.

"Nothing," I say.

"Josh, why have you got a breast reduction leaflet on your table? Do you have something you need to tell me?"

"It's Becky's," I say.

"Hmm, well, don't let Mum see it."

"Why not?"

"She doesn't believe in plastic surgery," says my sister. "She believes we should all love the body we were given. And talking of lovely bodies, when's Barclay coming round again?"

"His name's Lloyd," I say. "And if he does come round, it'll be when you're on lates!" My sister does two lates a week at

Sherlock Combs, the beauty salon where she works, although I don't call engaging in a bit of banter while you paint people's nails working.

"Oh, come on," she says. "Don't be a meanie."

"No," I say, "you'll corrupt him."

"You just think he's gonna like me more than you."

"Maybe..." I admit.

"Oh well," says my sister, examining her claw-like nails. "I guess I won't tell you my exciting news then."

Aargh, my sister is so irritating. "What news?" I say.

"Remind me," says my sister, "of your life goals."

"Huh?" I say.

"Go on," she says. "I know you love making lists of things. You even talk in lists these days."

"Er, excuse me," I say. "Number one... oh."

"Exactly," says my sister. "So come on. What are they?"

"Well, to be a... metal guitarist," I say.

My sister nods. "Right, and what do all metal guitarists have?"

"Guitars?"

"Aha. And...?"

"Long hair?"

"Fine. *And?*"

"Leather jackets?"

My sister sighs loudly and shakes her head. "Tattoos!" she says. "I thought you wanted a tattoo!"

"Of course I do," I say, "but I looked into it at Tattoos 'R' Us and they said I was too young."

"Yes well, Tattoos 'R' Us aren't the only tattoo place in South Croydon," announces my sister enigmatically.

"That's true," I say.

My sister leans forward and grins in my face. "Now, *when* did you say Lloyd's coming round again?"

10.30pm

Text from Ollie:

> **How the duck are we sporran to do this Mat. Homework. It's a loaf of ship!**

Guess he must have auto-correct on.

Thursday 7th October

7.15pm: Inner Sanctum

I spend several minutes signing petitions on Facebook against ferret cruelty and am in a bit of a low mood when Mum pokes her head round my door.

"Why aren't you going to Scouts?" she asks.

"Um, it was cancelled," I say.

"Really?" says Mum, looking surprised. "That's unusual. Wait a minute, you didn't go last week either!"

"Sean had an abseiling accident," I say. "A really bad one. He's been in hospital for weeks."

"Oh no!" says Mum. "Poor Sean. Did he break anything?"

"His arms, I think," I say. "And one or two of his legs."

"One or two!"

"Actually, one. Yes, it was just the left one. So that's good as you don't need that one as... er, much..."

I have no idea why I told such an over-the-top, bonkers lie.

At any rate, Mum fixes me with a very odd look before leaving.

Friday 8th October

8.35am: Eldritch Portal

Davey has come over so we can walk to college together. He is wearing a giant orange cagoule.

"Davey," I say. "Don't take this the wrong way, but that is a seriously questionable style choice."

"Huh?" says Davey.

I can't help but laugh. "You look like a giant satsuma!"

"Fine," says Davey, struggling out of the cagoule. "But if I get wet and catch a cold it'll be your fault."

"Davey," I say, as we start walking. "If you had an older sister and she wanted to go out with me, would you let her?"

"Of course," says Davey. "It would be nice. We could be a threesome. Oh er, not in that way, though... I mean um..."

"Right," I say. "It's just that my sister wants to go out with Lloyd."

Davey stops in his tracks and stares at me.

"What?" I say.

Davey resumes walking. "Um, well, it's just your sister is a bit... er..."

"Out with it, Davey," I say.

"Well, a bit... *full on.*"

I nod. That's actually a very diplomatic way of describing my sister. It's like saying a zombie is a bit under the weather.

"Then again," says Davey, as we cross the high street, "some men like to be dominated. Some people like to be walked all over. Literally!"

"Metaphorically," I say.

"No, literally," says Davey.

Ha, I don't think Davey knows the difference between literally and metaphorically. He only just scraped a pass in GCSE English.

Saturday 9th October

4.15pm: Inner Sanctum

I had an embarrassing trip to the park with Minty today. She would not stop barking at a perfectly pleasant pug in a tartan coat. I hope she isn't racist. She's also been known to bark at blonde women on television.

The pug's owners, an angry-looking elderly couple, gave me a 'control your dog' look. Little do they know, I have as much control over Minty's behaviour as I do over Middle Eastern peace negotiations. Less, maybe.

Anyway, I was so embarrassed that I tried to lose her for a few minutes by hiding behind a bin shaped like a frog. Needless to say, the little git sniffed me out, wagging her tail while simultaneously growling. If I ever have a dog it'll be a German Shepherd. I will call him Herman and he will be a model of canine behaviour; ready to race through fire, ice and bogs to save me if the need arises.

When I take Minty back to Ned's, he says, "Tell your mum I'll be thinking of her."

Why Ned tortures himself with thoughts of Mum, I don't

know. She'll never return the favour, at least not until he gets rid of his beer mats.

Sunday 10th October

2.00pm: Nan's house

Nan is introducing me to her friend Mavis who has come over to keep her company, and drink large quantities of Scotch, by the look of the half-empty bottle on the coffee table.

"This is my son," says Nan.

"Grandson, Nan," I say.

"What?"

"I'm your grandson."

Nan raises her hands. "Yes, my grandson! He's very good on the banjo."

"Guitar, Nan," I say. "I play the guitar."

"I like a bit of classical guitar," says Mavis.

"I play hard rock and metal," I say.

"I expect you do Music at college," Mavis goes on, before taking a swig of Scotch.

"No," I say. "I would've liked to, but my mum thought I should keep it as a hobby." And do all the insanely difficult subjects that have masses of exams and heaps of homework instead, I add, privately.

"I hope you're taking care of your mum," says Nan, suddenly deadly serious-looking. "She really needs you now, you know."

"Huh?" I say.

"My son plays the banjo!" announces Nan, suddenly smiling again.

I must tell Mum that Nan is losing it big time and also being corrupted by elderly ladies with an enthusiasm for hard liquor.

10.00pm: Inner Sanctum

I practise a bit of Metallica on the guitar, then do some Biology homework and a bit of dirt house building on Minecraft. Amazingly, I have my own PC now, thanks to Ned. It's second-hand and has a load of Hello Kitty stickers on the monitor which won't come off, but beggars must be losers, or something like that.

I go to draw my curtains before getting into bed. It's a clear sky tonight, so I take Ozzy out of his cage so he can see the stars. "Look," I say, "there's the plough."

Ozzy looks up where I'm pointing but wriggles a bit to get down. I guess you don't get many ferrets into astronomy; it's more a people thing. I put Ozzy on the bed and am just about to pull the curtain when I notice a movement on the little patch of grass/dirt beneath my window. There's a fox there, peering straight up at me. He's frozen in the light from the street lamp and probably scared, so I creep backwards from the window and turn off my light, but when I look back out again he's gone.

Monday 11th October

2.10pm: English

Yes! I got a B for my English essay (I hope I'm not peaking too early). Anyway, Andy said it was the most heartfelt piece of literature he'd ever read on footwear – I decided to hand in the one on my trainers after all. It just goes to show that you should trust your instincts and not let the fear of being hideously ridiculed stifle your creative impulses.

Also, I couldn't be arsed to write another essay.

6.55pm: Kitchen

"I need to know what he's like," says Maddie. "Are his folks laid-back and cool?"

My sister has trapped me in the kitchen after I casually mentioned to her that Lloyd may be coming round soon.

"Absolutely not," I say. "They are a highly religious, domesticated family. The sort of family that sits together of an evening, singing and baking cakes."

"I can bake cakes," says my sister. "I got a GCSE in Food Technology."

"Technically, a D is a fail," I remind her.

"I'll bake a Victoria sponge," says Maddie, ignoring this. "Or maybe some flapjacks, or cupcakes, or a Black Forest gateau!"

"Fine, Maddie," I say. "You've proven you know a lot of names for cakes. So now I've kept to my side of the deal, enlighten me as to how Lloyd coming over is supposed to help me get a tattoo."

Maddie grins and helps herself to one of my crisps. "After I tell you what I'm about to tell you," she says, "you're gonna think I'm the best sister eva!"

Unlikely.

Tuesday 12th October

5.00pm: Inner Sanctum

Davey, Ollie, Peter and me are sat on the floor of my Inner Sanctum. This is because Minty is asleep on the bed and only someone in possession of a stun gun or Ned's reinforced gloves would be prepared to move her. Downstairs, Mum and Ned are watching a romantic film together. I'm hoping some of it might rub off on Mum but I'm not holding my breath.

"How's it going with your olds?" I ask Peter.

"They were arguing again last night," Peter says.

"What about?" I say.

Peter shrugs. "I don't know. I put my headphones on and let Beyoncé drown them out. I ended up listening to 'Single Ladies (Put a Ring on It)' five times."

"If you like it..." sings Davey.

"Stop, Davey!" I say.

Ollie gets up and makes a move to sit on the bed but Minty starts growling so he thinks better of it and slumps back down on the floor. "So wassup wit' yo' sista n' Lloyd?" he says. "They like a thing?"

"I have agreed to help my sister get together with Lloyd," I say, "but only because she has promised to get me a tattoo."

"How's she gonna do that?" exclaims Peter.

"There's this Scottish tattooist coming into Sherlock Combs where she works," I say. "Six foot four. Massive muscles. Ginger hair. The works."

"Go on," says Davey.

"Well, he likes a certain service..."

"What?" they say simultaneously, eyes goggling.

"He likes his lashes tinted."

"Is dat one of dem euphemisms?" asks Ollie.

"No," I say. "His eyelashes are white and he hates them."

"Hmm, it's true: white lashes are an acquired look," agrees Peter.

"'Course, he's a bit embarrassed about the whole procedure," I go on. "It not being very macho. So my sister told him she'd do it when everyone else had gone home if he did me a tattoo."

"Yo' sister is da bomb!" exclaims Ollie.

"But hasn't this guy heard of mascara?" Peter says. "Some waterproof brands last ages and he could apply it in the comfort of his own home for a fraction of the cost."

"No, he hasn't," I say. "And don't you tell him!"

"Well," says Davey, getting to his feet. "Let's just hope he knows what he's doing. I've seen some pretty horrendous tattoos on the internet, I can tell you. Ow, my legs have gone dead..."

Suddenly Minty comes roaring off the bed in a snarling blur of teeth and fur.

"Whoa!" we say.

Davey somehow manages to scramble up on my desk at the other side of the room, sending pens and paper flying, while Minty barks at him furiously, all four feet coming off the ground at once.

"She's gonna rip my throat out!" cries Davey.

"Don't panic, Davey," I say. "I just have to get the reinforced gloves."

Wednesday 13th October

12.50pm: Canteen with Ollie and Peter

We are just about to tuck into our pizza and potato wedges (one of the better canteen offerings) when this Goth girl comes up, grabs one of my wedges and starts chewing on it.

"Er, can I help you?" I say, which I think is remarkably polite considering.

"It's me," says the Goth.

"Huh?" I say.

"Wow, great disguise!" says Peter. "Are you going to a fancy dress party?"

"No," says the Goth, now taking a whole handful of wedges.

"Um, excuse me!" I say, putting down my fork. "I don't know who you think you are..."

"I think I'm Becky!" says the Goth, dragging out a chair opposite and sitting down wearily.

And suddenly I realise that of course it's Becky. It's just that she's wearing an enormous black t-shirt, a long black skirt and masses of eyeliner. She's done something weird and quite scary to her hair too.

"Well," I say. "This is a surprise. Your hair – it's different!"

"No, it's the same hair I've always had," says Becky.

"It's slammin'!" says Ollie.

"Yeah, well, this new look is a way I can cover up my boobs," explains Becky. "Plus, as you know, I've always had a bit of a crush on Jared from 30 *Seconds to Mars*."

"Oh, me too," says Peter.

Ollie wipes his mouth. "Man, you don't wanna cover 'em up!"

he says, horrified. "They're like... assets."

"Yeah, right," says Becky. "Having two giant melons bobbing up and down when you walk is a real asset."

"Ain't no different to having a king-size banana and two plums," says Ollie, grinning. "And you don't hear me complaining!"

Becky gets up, grabs my few remaining wedges and turns away in a skirt-swishing huff.

"Nice one, Ollie," I say.

"What?" says Ollie.

5.15pm: Inner Sanctum

I haven't been on Facebook for a while as I was finding it a bit depressing. Everyone is always posting amazingly attractive pictures of themselves in amazingly sexy/macho poses at amazing parties where they are the absolute centre of attention and everything is just, like, totally amazing! The last picture I put up was of Ozzy lying on his back eating a grape. He looked dead cute, though. Kinda like an otter.

Anyway, now that I've had a bit of a digital detox, I thought I'd message Becky and check she's OK. However, just as I'm about to, I notice Ollie has updated his relationship status. Apparently, he's now in a relationship with someone called Rose Thorn. Surely that must be a joke name? Maybe it's code for 'someone I spoke to online who lives thousands of miles away and who I therefore have no chance of ever meeting'!

I see he's on Facebook so I message him.

Who's Rose Thorn? I ask him.

Chick I met

Is her name really Rose Thorn? I reply.

Yo

You meet on internet?

Nope, Pets at Home. He types.

You met at a pet shop???

Bongo puked in tha hamsta section and she cleaned it up

Nice! Is she hot?? I type.

There's a pause before Ollie resumes typing.

Is the sun red?

I don't think it is, is it?

Thursday 14th October

1.35pm: Canteen with Ollie, Davey and Peter

"Rose is an amazing kisser," says Ollie. "She's won loads of kissing competitions."

"Do kissing competitions actually exist?" I ask.

"Of course they do," says Ollie.

"They don't, do they?"

"No."

"Hmm, there's something different about you, Ollie," I say.

"He's not talking like a meth dealer any more," says Peter.

"That's it," I say. "You just said Rose is an amazing kisser rather than, 'Yo! Rose be one straight-up, pimped-out kissa!' How come?"

Ollie shrugs. "I had to get out of the habit. I accidentally said, 'Wassup, biatch!' to Rose and she wasn't impressed."

"You nutter!" laughs Davey.

"I'm still keepin' it real, though," says Ollie.

"Oh, sure," we say nodding. "Absolutely."

This seems to be all we can get out of Ollie regarding Rose for the moment so Davey says, "Are you getting your tattoo soon, Josh?"

"Not 'til my sister and Lloyd are officially an item," I say, "which hopefully won't be very long, although she might kill him first with her cooking."

"She should come to Scouts," says Peter happily. "We're making 'Fun Low-Fat Desserts' tonight!"

7.15pm: Scouts (after three-week suspension)

We watch Sean and the other Scout master, Anthony, demonstrate how to make a Knickerbocker Glory and are then let loose to have a go ourselves. There are tables laid out with all sorts of yummy things like fresh fruit, low-fat cream, sponge cakes and jugs of custard. Shame that, in about thirty seconds, it'll all be completely inedible. Anyway, I've decided that no matter what happens this evening I am not going to let that sad, pathetic lame-ass (Wentworth) get to me. I will just keep my head down and pretend he isn't here.

Someone taps me on the back. "Sean says I gotta join your group," says Wentworth.

Keep calm, Josh. Keep calm.

"Sure," I say, smiling. "That's fine. What dessert would you like to make?"

"A banana split," says Wentworth.

I give Wentworth a banana. And then another one. And then, even though I know it's really bad, one more.

"Er, I don't need three, moron," he says.

"Yes, you do," I say. "All the best banana splits have three bananas. Well-known fact. I used to work in a pub restaurant and banana splits were their speciality and they all used three large bananas. People went... bananas for them."

Wentworth shrugs but takes his bananas to the other end of the table.

"Can I make a banana split too?" asks Duncan, one of the younger, newer Scouts.

"Sorry," I say. "We're out of bananas; make a peach melba instead."

"But I wanted..."

"Make a peach melba!" I hiss.

I have decided to help the other Scout in my group, Tim, do a strawberry pavlova. Tim is a shy, nerdy kid who is probably only here because his mum worries about his social skills. He is one of those people who never gets noticed but I am determined that his pavlova will! There's a prize for best dessert and Tim's will be the best if it kills me. I grab a large meringue nest and get Tim to pump it full of cream from the aerosol.

"We'll decorate it really well," I tell him. "If we concentrate and work closely together we can do this, Tim. We can totally win!"

"Um, OK," says Tim.

Tim's pavlova is coming along a treat – literally! We've got an alternating orange and red theme going on which looks very professional and sophisticated. We just need to add some chocolate buttons, marshmallows, multi-coloured sprinkles and glitter.

"You're helping him way more than anyone else," says Wentworth, wandering over and nodding at Tim.

"No, I'm not," I say. "I halved Duncan's peaches."

"You haven't helped *me* at all," says Wentworth.

"You're older and more experienced in the ways of desserts."

"Just 'cause I said your girlfriend's a lezzer."

"Oh, don't start that again," I say. "Bring your bananas over here and I'll take a look."

"And everyone knows three bananas can kill a person!" cries Wentworth. "You want me DEAD!"

"What?" I say. "That's ridiculous!"

"Actually..." says Peter, who has chosen this moment to stick his nose in.

"Not now, Peter!" I say.

"You've always hated me, just 'cause I beat you at Monopoly," whines Wentworth.

"Oh, really? You said it was because my girlfriend's a lezzer a minute ago," I remind him. I am smiling while I say this in an effort to try and defuse things, but this seems to enrage Wentworth even more and he suddenly grabs Tim's pavlova and flings it at my chest! Luckily, it misses and hits me full in the face.

"Nooo!" cries Tim.

I don't know whether I am spurred on by Tim's mournful cry

or by the sudden realisation that Wentworth is such a puny git that I should be able to take him down easy. Whatever it is, I say a line I have only ever said in my dreams: "Come on then, if you think you're hard enough!"

Wentworth *does* think he's hard enough. He launches himself at my stomach head first and sends me crashing back into the table. Peaches, bananas and strawberries fly everywhere.

"Fight! Fight! Fight!" chant the Scouts, gathering round like depraved vultures.

I wipe custard off the seat of my trousers and look round to see Wentworth dancing about, fists raised. He's got a bloody hard head, I'll give him that. I feel winded and disorientated. Where are the frickin' Scout leaders when you need them? No doubt outside, puffing on their death sticks.

While I am thinking this, Wentworth is on me again. He takes me into an arm lock and we stagger off to the side of the hall together before I lose my balance and fall down onto a pile of tent poles. This makes a change from fruit, but hurts a whole lot more.

"Hold on, Josh," I hear Peter cry. "I'm going to get Sean."

But Peter doesn't get Sean because just as Wentworth is about to smash a pineapple in my face (spiky green end first), Peter leaps on his back and starts yanking his hair. Wentworth screams, turning this way and that in an attempt to throw Peter off. Meanwhile, I finally manage to stagger to my feet, but not without sending poles and small Scouts flying in all directions.

"Kill the bastard!" shrieks Peter who has now completely lost it.

I lunge out, grab Wentworth by the woggle and drag him to the ground. Then, even though I can hear Sean and Anthony yelling and running, I empty an entire two-litre carton of orange juice straight into his horrified face.

It proves to be the last activity I ever do at Scouts because Sean looks at me and yells: "Get out NOW and never come back!"

Friday 15th October

I have decided to give college a miss today as I have a swollen eye, a cut lip, a seriously bruised bum and a Biology test.

Saturday 16th October

4.35pm: Inner Sanctum

"What's that smell?" says Davey, crinkling his nose.

"It's Eau de la Ferret by Ozzy," I say.

Davey shakes his head. "What *will* they come up with next? Oh well, I brought you a banana cream doughnut from the 'Eat Immediately If You Don't Want To Die' section" says Davey, sitting on my bed and opening his bag. "Thought it'd cheer you up."

"Thanks, Davey," I say. I wish it had been apple filling inside as I'm kinda sick of bananas, but it was a nice thought.

Davey is wearing a purple t-shirt with a toucan on and some zebra-print jogging bottoms. I don't know if it's because I've had a serious head injury or what, but when I look at him from a certain angle, I start to hallucinate.

"How's Peter?" I ask. "Is his face OK?" Peter had received a few nasty scratches in the Wentworth debacle.

"He's covering them with his mum's foundation cream," says Davey. "You can hardly see them."

Davey gives me the Biology handouts I missed yesterday and shares a bit of gossip on Ollie. Davey thinks he spotted Rose in Pets at Home. She's about twenty and has gingery hair. He couldn't see a name badge, but she had very full, kissable lips and a woman was talking to her about Labrador digestive systems.

"That's her!" I say. "Was she hot?"

Davey considers. "About room temperature," he says. "There was a bit of excess facial hair but nothing a good-quality razor couldn't fix."

It is nice to see Davey but I wish Becky would visit, too. I texted her earlier to say how I'd been very badly beaten up. I was hoping she'd drop everything and rush over. But she hasn't.

Sunday 17th October

10.35am: Inner Sanctum

Text from Becky:

Sorry you were hurt, Josh. That was very brave of you standing up to that gang of horrible men to save that poor kitten.* Sorry I haven't seen you much but I'm in a bit of a shitty place right now. Will text when I feel better XX

It's a shame; I'm sure we could've cheered each other up. I could have played her my latest riff or we could've had another look through the breast reduction leaflets. I guess number one on my list of things to achieve (make progress with Becky) is off, at least for the time being.

*I told a bit of a white lie there!**
**OK. Black lie.

Monday 18th October

11.55am: College canteen

"Ha!" exclaims Ollie when he sees my face, which is still a bit blue and puffy. "A weedy little twelve-year-old did *that?*"

"He's thirteen," I say. "And thanks, you sure know how to make a person feel better."

"It just goes to show that violence is never the answer," says Davey, which is fair enough considering Davey's never been violent with anything other than a bag of crisps.

Peter wanders over with his tray. He is wearing a bright yellow beanie pulled down low over his forehead, presumably to hide Wentworth's scratches.

"Nice hat," I say.

"Ah thanks, Josh," says Peter, his eyes lighting up.

Sarcasm is lost on him.

Tuesday 19th October

4.50pm: Lounge, awaiting the arrival of Lloyd

"When did you say he's coming, again?" asks my sister.

I take a deep breath. "Five o'clock. He just has to go home and get his bass."

My sister is frantically collecting up her trashy magazines – all fake tans and celebrity cellulite. I wouldn't be surprised if she hadn't gone to the newsagents earlier and bought a couple of copies of the *Financial Times* and *New Scientist* to casually toss on the sofa.

"Oh yes, Lloyd. I am very into science, especially Chemistry. All those

chemicals are just so fascinating, aren't they?"

There's a smell of burning coming from the kitchen.

"Cakes are done," I say.

"Shit!" cries my sister, flying out of the room.

Yes, my sister has decided to bake. This is no cause for celebration, though, as I suspect her cakes will be more like weapons of mass destruction than mouth-watering delights.

The doorbell goes and I let Lloyd in.

"Mmm, something smells nice," he lies.

"Ah, yes," says my sister, materialising in the hallway in what looks suspiciously like an apron. "That'll be my chocolate-drenched raisin bran oatcakes. Would you like to try one?"

"Yes please!" says Lloyd.

"I'll pass," I say.

Lloyd receives what looks like a fossilised cowpat from my sister, and takes a big bite.

"I hope you've got dental insurance," I say.

There is silence while my sister gives me a glacier-like glare and Lloyd gnaws his way through the cow excreta.

"Mmm," he says, eventually swallowing. "Lovely."

"It's got raisins in," says my sister, "and bran and oats to make it extra healthy."

"It's delicious."

"Well," says my sister. "You lads better go do your music thing but maybe you'll come down later, *Lloyd*, for another cake or two?" Here my sister fixes me with a purposeful stare.

"Love to," says Lloyd.

"See you later, then," says my sister, smiling and twirling away in her apron.

"Your sister is very domesticated," says Lloyd as we go upstairs. "I like that in a girl."

"Er, yep," I say. I don't tell Lloyd that she's actually about as domesticated as a great white shark.

We spend the next two hours jammin' together with only short breaks for crisps and energy drinks. Lloyd brought four cans and has downed three of them himself. I was slightly worried he'd have a major burst of speed on the bass and I wouldn't be able to keep up, but other than a slight eye twitch, they don't seem to have had much effect. I gotta say it's pretty cool playing with someone else, and I can imagine it'd be even better playing in a band.

Anyway, now I am giving Lloyd and my sister their 'alone time' in the kitchen. I have no idea what they are talking about but there's a good deal of high-pitched giggling going on, not all of which is coming from my sister.

Wednesday 20th October

4.00pm: Bathroom, washing hair

My sister comes in just as I finish washing my hair in the sink. When my hair was short, it was easier to care for, but this is just one of those sacrifices you have to make for metal. Anyway, I have used Maddie's special 'Mane Event' anti-frizz shampoo, which can only be bought on the internet for a ludicrous sum of money. I am expecting a huge rant, not to mention physical violence, but she just smiles and says, "Don't forget to put the top back on that shampoo."

Why is my sister in such a good mood?

Could it be that she's in love?

Thursday 21st October

1.15pm: Canteen

I am just joining the queue in the canteen when Lloyd runs up to me and gives me a small white envelope before saying he has to go. I'm expecting it to be some kind of love letter for my sister but it actually has *my name* on the front so I rip it open. Inside is a handmade card with an angel sitting on a smiling pumpkin, which says:.

You are invited to an Alternative Halloween Party!

Hmm, what's an Alternative Halloween Party? I read on:

As Christians, we do not believe in the dark pagan ritual of Halloween. However, that doesn't mean we can't have fun! Join us for our alternative Halloween festivities celebrating all that's light in the world!

****PLEASE COME!****

From Lloyd.

PS Fancy dress as your favourite Bible character! (Optional.)

PPS You can bring someone but probably best if it's not your sister — Mum can be a bit weird about some girls.

PPPS As I said earlier – Please come!

Five minutes later, eating lunch with Ollie, Davey and Peter

"Shame it's not a regular Halloween party," says Ollie. "You could've gone as you are."

"Hilarious, Ollie," I say.

Davey gives Ollie a high five.

"Yeah, well, anyway," I go on, "which one of you is gonna come with me?"

There's a very loud silence.

"Um, sorry Josh," says Davey, "but it sounds a bit..."

Peter grimaces. "Um, a bit..."

"Crap," says Ollie.

"Fine," I say. "Well, thank you so much, wonderful friends. Remind me to make sure that next time you need some little favour doin'..."

"Dude, don't go," says Ollie.

"I *have* to," I say. "Lloyd sounded desperate. Oh God, it'll be all middle-aged tambourinists. I'll have nothing in common with any of them and have no one to talk to."

"Talk to Lloyd," says Ollie, who is starting to annoy me.

"Don't be ridiculous," I say. "He'll be busy being the host."

Davey says, "Well, maybe he's got a pet."

"Mm-hmm," I say. "And how exactly is that gonna help?"

"You can talk to the pet, stupid," says Davey. "When I visited my aunt and cousins in Inverness I got anxious 'cause I don't know them very well. I ended up spending an entire evening talking to their black and white cat, Elvis."

This is an idea. Not a good one, but an idea all the same.

"OK," I say. "That could work, I guess. Thanks."

7.00pm

No Scouts tonight (or ever again) as I am banned for life. Mum doesn't know yet. She thinks the injuries I sustained last week were from falling off my bike. Anyway, I may have to start going out every Thursday from 7.30pm to 9.30pm, wandering the streets in the cold and dark so she doesn't find out. Luckily, tonight she's going to see Nan.

Friday 22nd October

I can't go to Lloyd's party. I checked on Facebook and I'm pretty sure he doesn't have a pet!

Well, he has two goldfish, Megatron and Optimus, but there's no way I can spend all evening talking to them. That's too weird even for me.

He's coming over to jam tomorrow so I'll have to tell him the bad news.

I message Becky on Facebook to see how she is. She messages back to say:

My life is finished. Mum said no to boob job : (

Saturday 23rd October

2.30pm: Pushing Ned and Minty back from Tesco

"Me and this Lloyd guy want to start a band," I tell Ned.

"Good for you," says Ned. "Though remember it is simple to open a shop; another thing to keep it open."

"Um, right," I say.

"In the big shed at the bottom of my garden there's an old drum kit," Ned goes on, "left over from my Atomic Dwarf days. It'll be a bit cobwebby and dusty, but if you can clean it off and put it back together, you're welcome to it."

"Wow," I say. "Thanks. I wonder if Mum'll let me have it in my bedroom."

"Hmm," says Ned. "Tell you what, why don't you and your mate bring it in and practise in my front room?"

"Really?" I say.

"'Course. It'd be nice to have some young folks round the place. I remember when me and the guys first started out with Atomic Dwarf. We thought we were gonna take the world by storm."

"And you did," I say. "You got into the charts, Mum said."

"'Graveyard Raver' made it to number 92," says Ned nodding and looking wistful.

"Awesome," I say.

"Yeah," replies Ned. "Anyway, I've got a keyboard somewhere, too. Maybe even some old mic stands. In fact, if you take a look down in that shed, there's probably all sorts of stuff kicking around that you could use."

Ned then proceeds to tell me all about touch-responsive

keys, song sequencing, midi interfaces, adjustable mic clips, XLR cables and many other very impressive-sounding things.

I feel a sudden surge of gratitude for all his help and for a worrying few seconds I'm tempted to lean over and give him a hug or at least some kind of tap on the back. Luckily, Minty spots this and lunges at me violently.

Sunday 24th October

6.00pm: Ned's

I've been round Ned's all afternoon checking out the stuff in the shed. There's loads of it in there. I decided to start by cleaning the drum kit but it took me ages because I had to rescue about ten million spiders. Anyway, I now have a very clean and sparkling drum kit.

But no one to play it.

10.00pm

It's 10pm so me and Ozzy take a look outside for the fox. He's there, chewing his way through the seriously healthy stick-and-gravel muesli I put out earlier. I can't wait for it to all be gone so we can go back to Coco Pops for breakfast.

Monday 25th October

10.45am: Morrisons

Yes, half term. I don't think I have ever been so glad to get to the holidays. It's not that I don't like college. I actually like it far more than school (not difficult!) but the work is just such a lot harder.

Anyway, I am just loading my smoky bacon crisps, milk and bread onto the conveyor belt when who should violently punch me in the back but Lloyd.

Uh-oh, this could be tricky.

"So you're coming to the party, then?" he asks, dumping his energy drinks behind my stuff.

"Um," I say. "Er..."

Damn it, why do I never prepare my excuses in advance?

"There'll be evangelical outreach and non-alcoholic punch," goes on Lloyd.

"What's that?" I say.

"It's a mixture of lemonade, orange juice..."

"No, the evanjelly thing?"

"Oh, that's just where we go door-to-door offering people cookies in the shape of angels and telling them about Jesus."

"Um, Lloyd," I say. "It's very nice of you, but..."

Lloyd puts the divider between our shopping. "It's OK," he says. "I understand. I'm proud of my Christian faith but Mum can tend to... overdo things. I know it's not very cool."

"Well," I say, "don't ask me about cool. I'm certainly not the world expert on cool. LOL. Ha! See what I mean; I said LOL out loud!"

I notice the checkout lady giving me a pitying look.

"Anyway, I can tell you what *is* cool," I say. I go on to tell Lloyd about all the stuff in Ned's shed. The mic stands, cables, keyboard, effects pedals and, of course, the drum kit.

"Awesome!" says Lloyd.

We pay for our stuff and wander outside. "'Course, what we need now are some other band members," I say. "I don't suppose you know any?"

"Only a couple of tambourinists and my cousin," says Lloyd. "But *you* must have some mates you can ask?"

"Oh yeah, sure," I say. "No problem. I got *loads* of people I can ask."

I don't.

11.30am: Davey's house

"Hi," says Davey. "Didn't expect to see you today. Wassup?"

"Davey," I say, "I need to ask you something."

"Er, OK," says Davey, inviting me into his lounge.

I make myself comfy on Davey's sofa.

"Have you ever considered playing the drums?"

"Huh? Well, no, not really. Why?"

"Because I actually think you'd be really good at it. You've got natural rhythm."

"Have I?" says Davey, looking pleased.

"Yes, and playing the drums is very good exercise. Did you know that a one-hour drumming session can burn off a million calories?"

"Wow! Really?"

"Also, drummers are very sexy. Girls always go for the drummers in a band."

"I thought they went for the lead singer," Davey says.

"Nope, drummers all the way," I say. "They like people who are good with their hands."

Davey grins.

Tuesday 26th October

3.45pm: Ollie's house

"Ollie," I say, "you know you used to play a bit of piano?"

"Yeah, when I was about nine," says Ollie. "It was boring as shit."

"Yes, but have you ever considered playing *keyboards*?"

"No."

"You should," I say. "Chicks always go for the keyboardist in bands."

"I think you mean the lead singer," says Ollie.

"Nope, definitely the keyboardist and, you know, you can never have too many chicks hanging around."

Ollie tilts his head to one side and nods thoughtfully.

Two down, one to go!

Wednesday 27th October

5.10pm: Peter's house

"What is the scariest and loudest noise you can make?" I ask Peter.

"I beg your pardon?" says Peter.

"Say *erraaarrgh*!"

"Why?" says Peter, narrowing his eyes at me.

"What's with all the questions?" I say. "I just need to see if you can say Erraaarrgh really loud and scarily? It's a perfectly sensible request."

"Is this some kind of weird sex thing?" says Peter. "Does Becky like it when you growl at her?"

"No," I say. "Jesus! Everything isn't always about sex, Peter. Besides, I told you, me and Becky aren't together at the moment; she's in a shitty place right now."

"OK. *Erraaarrgh*," says Peter.

"Is that the best you can do?" I say. "That was crap."

"Fine!" says Peter. He takes a deep breath, sits up straight and yells: *"ERRRAAAAARRRGH!!!!"*

Jesus! The noise he makes is inhuman. Part scream, part growl, it sounds like it has been spewed from the very depths of hell. I put my fingers in my ears to see if they're bleeding. They aren't, but there is a crack in the ceiling that I'm sure wasn't there before.

"How was that?" asks Peter.

"It was, um, pretty good," I manage. "Do you fancy being lead singer in my band?"

"OK," says Peter. "Guys always go for the lead singers in bands."

"Yes, they do," I say.

Thursday 28th October

3.30pm: Inner Sanctum

There's good news and there's bad news, I message Lloyd over Facebook.

Good news first, he messages back.

We have our band. I type.

Great! Bad news? He asks.

None of them have any musical ability whatsoever!

Friday 29th October

6.00pm: Inner Sanctum

I reach under my bed amid the stray socks and decaying tissues for my leather-bound notebook. I open it up at my most recent list and place a big decisive tick next to point number two – make new friends and form a band. Result!

So, we are all going round Ned's a week tomorrow to practise. In the meantime, I'm gonna go through more of Ned's old equipment and Ned is gonna give Davey some drumming lessons.

To be honest, neither Davey, Ollie nor Peter have much interest in being in a band and they all think metal is crap. But they'll basically do anything if they reckon it'll help them get laid. Of course, it's gonna take a lot of practice for the others to get up to speed. However, I already have some lyrics and an excellent name for the band so at least we won't have to waste any time thinking about that!

Saturday 30th October

4.15pm: Ollie's Inner Sanctum

"Why *Josh* and the Evil Goats?" says Peter. "I'm lead singer so it should be *Peter* and the Evil Goats."

"And why evil?" replies Davey. "I know it's metal and all that, but goats aren't evil. They're cute and very intelligent."

"And why *goats*?" asks Ollie. "If we're gonna have an animal it should be one everyone likes, like Labradors."

"Right," I reply. "So you're suggesting we call ourselves Peter and the Intelligent Labradors?"

Peter's eyes light up. "I like it!" he says.

6.20pm: Lounge

Lloyd has decided to risk his mother's disapproval and has invited Maddie to his Alternative Halloween Party instead of me. This isn't quite the hot date Maddie had in mind, but she's keen to impress his family and is going dressed as Mary Magdalene. This is so appallingly inappropriate it is almost funny. Anyway, she has found an old tablecloth at the back of the airing cupboard and she and my mum are desperately trying to make some kind of cloak/dress/shroud out of it.

"If this date goes well," Maddie tells me, when Mum goes to the kitchen for some scissors, "I'll talk to Angus next time he comes for his lashes and get you an appointment."

"Cool," I say. "Thanks."

"I'm hoping to entice Lloyd back here after we've made everyone right with Jesus and show him some *real* trick or treats."

I wish my sister wouldn't say stuff like this. It totally creeps me out.

Sunday 31st October

7.00pm

Text from Peter:

7.10pm

Another text from Peter:

7.35pm: Peter's lounge

What Peter really means by 'exclusive' is rubbish. There are five of us here: Peter, me, Davey, Ollie and Peter's baby brother, Julian. I am wearing the same zombie mask I wear every year. Davey has a bandage wrapped round his head. Ollie has painted his face orange. I'm not sure why. And Peter is wearing a cat mask, whiskers and black jumpsuit. Little Julian is a zombie like me. Although, a much better one, it must be said.

"Are you a zombie too?" he asks.

"God, no," I say. "I wouldn't be seen dead dressed as a zombie."

Everyone starts laughing except Julian, who looks a bit put out.

Anyway, Peter's mum has laid on a selection of party food: mini Swiss rolls with slime-green icing; cupcakes with severed marzipan fingers sticking out the top; gloopy, blood-red tomato juice. It's all pretty good, actually. And there are plastic bats and spiders hanging from the curtain poles and three giant pumpkins in the windows with faces that are gonna seriously traumatise any sensitive kids who come round.

"Your mum did a great job with this at such short notice," I say.

"Well, Dad's working late so I think she wanted to make the most of him not being here; she's always really liked Halloween," says Peter.

"I wish my mum did," I say. "Last year, she went out to bingo with a couple of the old ladies she cleans for and left me home alone with no sweets. I had to give people digestive biscuits and, when they ran out, cream crackers."

"Cream crackers?" says Davey.

"It was either that or make them a cup-a-soup."

8.00pm: Random streets

We take Julian trick-or-treating for about twenty minutes or so, thankfully not meeting my sister and Lloyd on our travels.

"Once I get my car we can drive round these streets for sweets," says Ollie. "No more of this walking shit."

"Mmm," I say.

Meanwhile, Peter is constantly tweeting:

People on Gregory St are sooo mean! #TrickorTweet

Foam bananas yummy! #TrickorTweet

Nooo... Getting colder and a few spots of rain. #TrickorTweet

Fang lost somewhere near Park Road, pls RT / tweet if found!

#TrickorTweet

9.15pm: Peter's Inner Sanctum

Julian takes his sweets (and himself) off to bed so we can talk about adult matters like whether Mrs Parson's nipples were visible beneath her leopard-print onesie (consensus was yes) and what colour front door is best (no consensus).

I get a freaky text from my sister:

About to find out if thing they say about black men is true!

Why did she have to text me that? She is seriously messed up. Poor Lloyd. I can't believe I have sacrificed him to her demonic ways for the sake of a tattoo.

Peter switches on his computer and logs into Facebook. I am almost too scared to look in case my sister has posted something disgusting on my wall, but she hasn't.

Davey wants to play Minecraft but Peter says it's impossible to build a nicely furnished flat with a bunch of cubes, so we spend an hour watching him on *The Sims* instead. I wouldn't mind but in my opinion *The Sims* just simulates everything that's rubbish in life, like having to go to work and school and the toilet, etc. Peter is an expert, though. He has even made his own Sims tutorials for YouTube. Yes, he is *that* obsessed.

After a long time of watching Peter fine-tune his Sims' eyebrows, Davey and Ollie make their excuses and go. I should probably head off too but I don't want to barge in on anything at home so I decide to stay a bit longer. Hopefully, by the time I finally get back, Lloyd will have gone, or at least got his trousers back on.

We say goodbye to Ollie and Davey, and Peter starts working on his Sims' forehead height. Not knowing what else to do, I take a look along his bookshelves.

And that's when I see it, the book that was in Peter's bag a few weeks ago: *An Amateur Witch's Guide to Casting Spells*!

Peter is so engrossed in *The Sims* that I could set fire to his bed and he wouldn't notice, so I quietly open the book at the place he's marked with a strip of paper, and read:

A spell to make him yearn for your love

Woah! This is hilarious. I check to see if Peter is still oblivious. He is.

Cast this spell as the moon waxes full, says the book. What does that mean? God knows. I read on...

You will need:

Some black ribbon

At least two items of clothing from the one you desire

At least three items in regular usage by the one you desire

Three silver coins

Black candles

I am about to find out what you need to do with all these things when Peter says, "Do you think he looks better with a pointy chin or one that's more square?"

Luckily, he doesn't look round while I silently slide the book back in the bookshelf and wander over.

"Square," I say. "It gives him a more rugged look."

"Yes," says Peter. "He's quite handsome. He looks a bit like you, doesn't he?"

"Er," I say.

Monday 1st November

11.30am: Kitchen

My sister is humming as she makes herself a sandwich and she is wearing her smug face, which always annoys me.

"So," I say, "seeing as you've now completely corrupted my friend, I'm expecting to have an appointment set up pretty soon with the tattoo dude."

My sister smiles. "Honestly, Josh, you are so gullible! I had a nice time with Lloyd but nothing *dodgy* went on."

"Well... that's good," I say. "So are you seeing him again?"

"I'm thinking about it," says my sister as she dollops on the mayonnaise. "He's very cute but, to be honest, he *is* a bit young. I think I need someone more experienced to, shall we say, feed the fevers of my erotic fantasies!"

Erotic fantasies? Good grief!

Anyway, while it's a relief that Maddie's having second thoughts about Lloyd, I'm worried it might mean our deal is off.

"So about this tattoo..." I begin.

"Next time Angus is in, I'll speak to him about it."

"And when will that be?"

"Probably quite soon," says my sister. "Eyelash tinting lasts about four to six weeks but some people like to build on their tints to keep the look from fading. Also, it depends if he's been using oil-based cleansers, moisturisers or foundation."

"Enough already," I say, holding up my hand. "Jesus. I don't need to know all the gory details!"

Tuesday 2nd November

7.30pm: Ned's, with Davey

I have been cleaning and setting up mic stands in the front room while Ned has spent the last two hours giving Davey a crash course in drumming. (Crash being the operative word!) I still can't believe I'm on my way to achieving my aim of getting a band together!

"Oh dear," says Davey, as another drumstick goes somersaulting across the room, narrowly missing Minty's head.

"Not a problem," says Ned. "Everyone does that when they're starting out."

"I'm sorry about chipping your drumsticks," says Davey.

"Ah," Ned waves his hands. "I can always buy more."

"And for breaking your vase."

"What's a guy like me want with flowers?"

"And the, er, television."

"Er, well, yes, that was a bit of a nuisance."

Ned is actually looking quite pale so me and Davey say goodbye and make our way home. I have decided not to tell Davey (or anyone else) about Peter's spell book. We all have secret, pervy, weird stuff going on in our lives. Well, I don't, but a lot of people do. Besides, I want us to concentrate all our efforts on the band.

Wednesday 3rd November

2.35pm: Kitchen

I am starving today as I didn't have enough money to get anything from the canteen and the Seriously Reduced section in the supermarket was being dominated by an impenetrable wall of old ladies. Twice I got elbowed in the guts as I tried to glimpse the offers.

I'm guessing there will be nothing in our fridge, but I'm

wrong. There *is* something in the fridge and it's something pretty amazing. I s'pose I should ask Mum first, though.

I close the fridge and my stomach gives a WTF rumble.

OK, so it can't hurt if I just have a little bit...

5.30pm: Inner Sanctum, suffering from acid reflux

"Josh, come down here," Mum yells from up the stairs.

"Hi," I say, smiling. "Everything OK?"

"Where's the cheesecake that was in the fridge?"

"What cheesecake?" I say.

"The big chocolate cheesecake that was in the fridge. The one I was going to take to Mrs Harper for her eightieth birthday party."

"I have no idea," I say, shrugging. "Sorry. No idea at all."

My mum puts her hands on her hips and stares at me with her passive-aggressive look. Actually, it's more aggressive-aggressive.

"Josh!"

"Um, well, Maddie and that slightly overweight friend of hers, Darla, were around earlier," I blurt out. "They spent a long time in Maddie's' s bedroom with the door shut."

My mum sighs and rubs her forehead. "I do not need this stress right now," she says. "I've got enough worries as it is!"

"What worries?" I ask.

"It's nothing," says Mum.

I make my way back upstairs guiltily. If the saturated fat doesn't kill me, my sister probably will.

Thursday 4th November

4.20pm: Walking home from college with Davey and Peter

Davey tells us he's been doing loads of drumming practice.

"I think it's helping with my anxiety," says Davey. "When I get anxious I just beat the hell out of my parents' sofa. Of course, with cushions you don't get the same vibe as you do with cymbals, snares or toms. But with a little improvisation using a baking tray and some Tupperware containers you can make a surprisingly authentic sound."

"I can imagine," I say, which is a complete lie.

"Anyway, the good news is my parents are getting me a proper drum set for Christmas," goes on Davey. "So I can practise at home as well as at Ned's."

"Really?" says Peter. "Wow!"

"Yeah, a complete full size, five-piece set. Black and silver. It comes with some spare drumsticks and a useful beginner's DVD."

I gotta admit this is great news and I'm really glad Davey has taken to the drumming. Of course, he's a seriously spoilt brat but he hasn't let this turn him into a complete dick so I guess I can forgive him.

Friday 5th November

10.05pm: Inner Sanctum

I am exhausted. Davey, Ned and me spent the entire evening setting up Ned's front room ready for our first sesh with the whole band tomorrow. I hope we didn't tire Ned out too much. Sometimes I forget about his arthritis and the fact that he's really old (in his fifties). Anyway, I'm excited about the band but also a bit worried. What if we suck?

Well, of course we're gonna suck. At least *they* will. I won't, because I'm the proverbial Head of Shred!*

It's Guy Fawkes Night tonight and Ozzy doesn't like the fireworks so I've let him burrow under my duvet. I wish he would keep still so I could warm my feet up on him. It's bloody freezing in my Inner Sanctum. My toes are like frozen prawns.

Saturday 6th November

1.30pm: Ned's front room

Ned has offered to be our manager, which is excellent news as Ollie et al. are far more likely to listen to him than they are to me. He has also let us completely invade his front room. It is now heaving with amps, cables, mic stands, a drum kit, guitars, a keyboard, a computer, beer (4.5% proof) and an enormous bowl of smoky bacon crisps which he knows are my favourites! Minty is having a major sulkfest over her personal space being invaded but she has to realise she can't always get her own way.

"Ha!" says Lloyd, cracking open a beer. "If Mum could see this!"

"She not a fan of alcohol?" I ask.

"You could say that. Though she'd probably be pleased I'm having somethin' other than energy drinks for once."

Hmm, this is actually something I've been meaning to ask Lloyd about.

Head of Shred (AKA Guitar Ninja). Shredding is an insanely fast soloing technique involving sweep-picked arpeggios, diminished and harmonic minor scales, rapid finger-taps and general guitar craziness such as whammy-bar 'dive bombs'. Don't say I never teach you anything!

"How many of those do you drink?" I say.

"Oh, not many," says Lloyd. "Four or five."

"A week," I say, nodding.

"A day," says Lloyd.

"A day!"

Lloyd sighs. "Your sister told me I should cut down. Sometimes my mind's so active, I'm up all night balancing chemical equations."

"That is... worrying," I say. I'm about to say more but Lloyd looks so fed up that I bottle out (no pun intended) and change the subject.

"So, um, how did it go with my sister?"

"Oh, pretty good," says Lloyd. "I think she's friendzoned me though, 'cos she wasn't sexually predatory once."

I'm about to tell Lloyd he's had a lucky escape when all thoughts of Maddie are pushed aside by Davey thrashing around on the drums like someone battling a horde of wasps. He is joined by Ollie, who starts playing 'Greensleeves' with insane amounts of vibrato, and Peter, who tries to sing along using made-up words.

"OK, OK!" yells Ned, coming into the room and restoring calm. "How about we all try playing the same song? Let's start with a simple old-time classic. 'Born to be Wild' by Steppenwolf."

We print out the chords and lyrics from the internet and two hours later we can play the first eight bars, albeit at a much reduced speed and with quite a few stops, while Davey retrieves his drumsticks from wherever he's flung them.

By this time Ned is pouring out his fourth beer and rubbing his forehead quite a lot, so I suggest we call it a day.

"So," says Ned as we pack up to leave, "have you decided what you're going to call yourselves?"

Hmm. I'd been putting off thinking about this since our last conversation on the subject.

"Not really," I say, going to get my coat which Minty has decided to lie on. She growls but I manage to poke her off with the end of a drumstick.

"How about we name ourselves after Minty?" says Lloyd. "But rather than The Yorkshire Terror we'd be The Croydon Terrors?"

"I'm not sure," I say. "It sounds a bit like a group for naughty toddlers."

"Josh wants to get goats in somewhere," Peter tells Ned.

"The London Goats!" exclaims Davey.

"No!" I say. "Honestly, Davey, you just don't get it, do you?"

"Terror Goat, then!" says Davey, rolling his eyes.

"Already taken."

"Evil Goat, Bad Goat, Sexy Goat," says Davey.

"Sexy Goat??"

"Goat Fiend, Rotten Goat, Rancid Goat, Gay Goat..." Davey goes on.

"Hold on," I say, "what did you say before Rotten Goat?"

"Goat Fiend," says Davey.

"Oh my God!" I say. "It's brilliant!"

"Really?" says Davey.

I watch through my fingers while Ned checks the internet to see if Goat Fiend is already a band.

"Nope, seems to be available," he says.

Fantastic.

We are Goat Fiend!

Sunday 7th November

3.30pm: Inner Sanctum

I spend a lot of time slaving over my Maths homework, which is insanely difficult, and spend even more time designing a logo for Goat Fiend. Luckily, as the name is quite short, it shouldn't involve too much pain getting it added to my Ozzy/Children of Bodom/Skull & Scythe tattoo.

Actually, maybe when we get really good (about twenty years' time) we could write to Children of Bodom requesting to be their support band! We could travel round the world in their tour bus and, in between the almost constant parties, girls and booze, we could have awesome jammin' sessions lasting whole days at a time. If that ever happens, I can finally say my life has begun. Until then, it's back to Maths homework.

6.15pm

Peter messages me on Facebook to say:

> Have put a bid on studded leather body suit on eBay. Ends in two days. Wish me luck! #Petersleathers

Shit. I may have to put a bid on so he doesn't get it.

Monday 8th November

10.15pm: Inner Sanctum window

The fox is there again, looking up at my window. Ozzy spots him and shows his appreciation by digging his claws sharply into my arm and making dooking noises.

In less than a minute the fox has demolished the muesli and

is looking up at me for seconds (clearly the poor thing has been driven half mad by starvation), so I put Ozzy on the bed and go downstairs to get more.

"Where are you going with that?" asks Mum as I sneak back upstairs with the box.

"Um, I just thought..."

"Do not feed that fox!" cries Mum. "*Especially* not with that. That's good, healthy food. It was very expensive!"

"Well, God knows why," I say. "It tastes like something you'd use to line Ozzy's cage. Why can't we have Coco Pops as usual?"

"Tell me you haven't been giving that to the fox," says Mum, ignoring this.

"Um," I say.

"Josh, you are constantly wasting money," says Mum. "First the cheesecake and now this. And don't think I don't know you've been banned from Scouts. Getting into fights, indeed. As if I don't have enough to worry about at the moment!"

This is the second time Mum's come out with this recently so I say, "What have you got to worry about?" And then because I'm a bit pissed off I add, "You're not the one with loads of nightmarishly difficult homework. And besides, if you would let Ned move in, then we'd have loads of money but no, you'd rather give me a hard time about some silly muesli."

"Give *you* a hard time?" cries Mum. "Ha, you have no idea!"

"Hard times aren't exclusive to you, Mum. You don't have the, er, what's the word? Scrabble... Monopoly! You don't have the monopoly on hard times!"

Mum doesn't say anything. She just snatches the box of muesli from my hand and walks away.

Tuesday 9th November

10.20am: College grounds – mid-morning break

I meet Ollie on a bench at the far side of the college grounds. He appears to be drinking a can of lager.

"All right?" he says and we high five.

"Ollie," I say, nodding towards the can. "It's like ten o'clock in the morning."

"Late breakfast," says Ollie.

"Can I have a swig?" I say, sitting down.

Ollie hands the can over.

"My mum had a right go at me last night," I say.

Ollie nods. "They do that sometimes."

"She is *so* moody!"

"Who's moody?" asks Peter, wandering over.

"Oh, no one," I say.

Peter shrugs and forces me to budge up. "Well, I didn't get the body suit on eBay," he says sadly.

"Oh," I say. "That's a shame." Things are looking up.

"I have put 'watches' on lots of other leather items though, including a pair of studded red leather trousers with matching biker's gloves."

Things *were* looking up.

6.30pm: Kitchen table doing Biology homework

Mum passes me my fish finger butty and sits down opposite me. "Sorry I've been a bit distant lately," she says.

"S'OK," I say, shrugging.

"College a bit tough at the moment, is it?"

"Aha."

"If you ever want to... you know, talk about anything."

"OK. Thanks," I say, not taking my eyes off my book.

"Actually, Josh, there is something I've been meaning to..."

"Mum, sorry, but I can't talk now. I have to get this homework done. It's due in tomorrow. Plus, I've got a Maths test to revise for."

"OK, love," she says, getting back up. "Try not to let your dinner get cold."

Honestly, parents. One minute, they're biting your head off and the next, they're wanting cosy chats.

Mother of My Destruction

O my mother, bringer of strife

Mistress of pain and oppression

Thou hath the power to wreck my life

Thou smile doth mask thy aggression

Hark! Your spirit! It bleeds me dry

Your questions? They chill me to death

Begone, foul mother, gone from my life

Give me peace til I take my last breath

From the album: *Bloody Relatives* by Goat Fiend

Hmm, powerful and tragically gothic, with a touch of *Lord of the Rings*. I'm quite pleased with those.

Wednesday 10th November

8.35am: Walking to college with Davey and Peter

"Damn," says Peter. "I've left my pencil case at home."

I sigh loudly. "Peter, if you spent less time worrying about your hair and eBay bidding, you'd have more time to pack your college bag properly."

Peter ignores this good advice and asks, "Can you lend me a pen, Josh?"

"Fine," I say, wearily opening my bag.

"And a pencil? HB, if possible."

"Right."

"And a ruler."

"Why don't you take the whole damn pencil case?" I say.

"OK," says Peter, making a grab for it.

"No!" I say, pulling it back. "What will I use if you do that?"

God, some people are so needy. Plus, I notice he never asked to borrow Davey's stuff.

Thursday 11th November

9.30pm: Inner Sanctum

I notice the fox is outside again. He wouldn't win any prizes for his tail – I've seen better bristles on Nan's chin. I put Ozzy on the windowsill so he can look down at his friend while I go to get the fox something. In the kitchen I cut off a few slices of cheese and creep back upstairs. I can't afford to let Mum see me doing this again; she will totally blow a gasket. Whatever a gasket is.

As I make my way along the landing to my Inner Sanctum, I can actually hear Mum and Maddie talking in Mum's bedroom. Shit! Maddie sounds like she's crying.

I edge quietly down the landing a bit.

"You have to tell him," Maddie says.

"I'll tell him in the morning," says Mum.

"Tell me what?" I say, appearing in the doorway.

Mum has her overnight bag open on the bed and is putting stuff in.

"What's going on?" I say. "Where are you going?"

"It's OK, Josh," says Mum. "I'm just popping into hospital. I'll be back the day after tomorrow."

"Why?" I say. "I don't understand..."

"Mum has cancer," says Maddie. "She didn't want to worry you, but I kept telling her you have to know."

I sit down on the edge of the bed and listen while Mum tells me that she has to have a small operation. The cancer is about a fifth of the size of her left breast and they are going to take it out. They also need to remove some lymph nodes under her arm, just to check it hasn't spread.

"When did you find out?" I ask.

I hear Maddie sigh and Mum says, "I've only known for definite for a few days but I've been going for tests and appointments for a while now."

"Oh," I say. "Right. But everything's going to be OK, isn't it?"

"Yes, of course," says Mum. "You know what a tough cookie I am!"

"And you'll definitely be home the day after tomorrow?"

"Absolutely," says Mum, smiling. "Now you'd better get to bed, Josh. You've got college in the morning."

I suddenly become aware of the cheese in my hands. It's gone all soft and manky. Mum gives me a big smile and I go back to my bedroom and toss it out the window. I feel really bad because I haven't been that nice to Mum recently. I open the leather-bound notebook, cross out the word *Mother* in the 'Mother of My Destruction' lyrics and put the word *Sister* in instead. I would cross them all out, but they are too good to get rid of entirely.

I then go to the window to watch for the fox but he is nowhere to be seen. Hopefully he'll be back soon.

Friday 12th November

1.15pm: College canteen

"Don't you want that?" Davey asks as I prod my burger and chips.

"Not really," I say.

"Can I have it?"

I pass my plate over to Davey.

Should I tell my friends about my mum? She will be having her operation soon. She and my sister got the taxi to the hospital at ten o'clock this morning. I wish I could've gone too, but Mum didn't want me to miss any lessons.

"You OK?" asks Peter.

"Yeah, fine," I say.

7.15pm: Inner Sanctum

Maddie says that she spoke to the hospital on the phone and they said the operation went well. I ask Maddie if she thinks Mum'll be all right and she says, "Yes, of course."

We put a pizza in the oven for our tea but I'm still not that hungry and don't eat much of it. I hope the fox likes olives.

Saturday 13th November

1.15pm: Mum's Inner Sanctum

Mum is home and in bed. Her arm is bruised and she can barely move her shoulder. She says she'll be fine though, once she's had time to get over the operation. Unfortunately, we have to wait up to two weeks to find out whether the cancer has spread.

I take Mum some cream of chicken soup with a side of crisps, as we are out of bread. Annoyingly, on the way up the stairs, I trip on one of my sister's stupid stilettos and spill a load. Luckily, our carpet is brown so it rubs in OK.

Mum nods towards the bedside cabinet and says to leave the soup there as she will eat it later. I'm about to say that it'll be cold then but her eyes are already drooping, so I grab a few of the crisps before making my way back downstairs.

Aargh! Damn my sister's shoes! Who leaves stilettos on a staircase, FFS...? Apart from someone plotting a murder, of course...

You plotted my downfall*

You wanted me dead

*literally!

Neck broken, spleen ruptured

The carpet stained red

Your weapon was simple

No crossbow or blade

No anti-tank rifle

Nunchuk or grenade

No assassin was poised

To attack with kung fu

But left high on the stair

Was your stiletto shoe

From the album: *Deadly and Unusual Weapons* by Goat Fiend

Cool.

6.30pm: Kitchen

Maddie says she might try and cook Mum something special tonight to try and boost her appetite a bit.

I say, "Well, whatever you do, don't bake her any cakes!" (*Another* deadly and unusual weapon!) Actually, I've just read through my deadly and unusual weapons lyrics and they are crap. I hope I'm not losing my touch.

Sunday 14th November

4.25pm: Ned's front room with Lloyd, Davey, Ollie and Peter

We need a new song to practise so, in the spirit of inclusion, I ask if anyone has any ideas. No one has, so I suggest 'Paranoid' by Black Sabbath. It doesn't have a keyboard part but Ollie says he'll improvise. I'm actually having serious suspicions about Ollie's musical ability. I think he might be quite good!

Ned helps us sort out the sound settings and demonstrates some of the trickier drum sections for Davey. After several hours of practising, I can see we are definitely getting better.

"I gotta say, since this band thing started, I've been practising just about every spare minute," says Lloyd. "I feel really committed, you know."

"Me too," says Davey.

"That's great," I say. "I mean, really..." Then I stop. Something terrible has happened – my voice has gone weird and my eyes are a bit prickly. "Um," I say. "Back in a sec."

In the bathroom, I splash my face and blow my nose. I don't know why I'm feeling so pathetically emotional. I stare at my reflection in the mirror. Is it a hormonal thing? Am I unstable? Anyway, I somehow manage to pull myself together and head back. In the lounge, Ollie is putting on his huge Hawaiian windbreaker and snapback cap. It's not really the sort of thing you'd expect a death metal keyboardist to wear, but it's early days – before the month is out his wardrobe will be filled with Metallica t-shirts!

"Has anyone seen my beanie?" I say, looking around. "My nan knitted it and Mum'll kill me if I've lost it."

The others shake their heads.

"You coming?" says Davey.

"Nah, you go on," I say. "I'll catch yer later."

I go and get Ned and we spend about ten minutes looking for my hat, without success. Ned even lifts Minty up so I can see if she was sitting on it, but she isn't, which is kind of a relief. I do, however, spot Davey's drumming book, which I stuff in my bag to give him at college.

"Give your mum my love, won't you," says Ned as I'm about to leave. "And tell her I hope she's feeling better soon."

"Sure," I say, smiling.

7.00pm: Inner Sanctum

Being a bit bored, I decide to have a look through Davey's *Drumming for Dummies* book. I don't get far though because tucked inside is an A4 sheet of folded paper. I open it up:

Rules for me

Ways to combat anxiety in social situations:

1. Think before I speak! Will I regret what I say later? Will it make me sound rude, stupid, high on drugs, etc.?

2. Look at people's faces when they talk, but not at their teeth.

3. Don't be TOO quiet. However, remember that not speaking is better than saying something stupid (see the first point).

4. Ask a few questions. Good one is: "Doing anything nice this weekend?" Unless it's Monday or Tuesday in which case say — "Doing anything nice this evening?"

Unless it's 10pm or later, then say —
"Doing anything nice tomorrow?"

5. For an easy conversation starter,
   compliment their clothing, e.g. "I like
   your shoes." But don't make it seem like
   you really love their shoes or they may
   think you have a weird shoe fetish!

6. Laugh if they say something that is
   meant to be funny, even if it isn't.
   But don't laugh when they are trying to
   be serious. Also don't overdo the fake
   laugh or laugh weirdly, squeak, snort,
   etc.

7. Telling jokes is good but think
   carefully because some things can be
   offensive. If in doubt, DON'T RISK IT.

I fold the paper up and throw it in my bin. It'd be way too embarrassing to give it back to him. Besides, he's probably got a copy on his computer.

Monday 15th November

4.35pm: Hallway

I have only just got back from college when the doorbell rings. I'm expecting to have to make excuses to a double-glazing salesman or someone offering to resurface our drive* so I am pleasantly surprised when it's Becky.

"Hi!" I say. "Come in."

Becky is wearing black leggings and a purple jacket with furry cat ears on the hood. She is looking very cute, in a morbid kind of way. I wonder if she knows about the formation of Goat Fiend and is going to ask to get back with me because

* Luckily, I do have a fail-safe, pre-prepared one for this: "Sorry, we are moving to Russia in three days." Genius!

of my imminent fame?

"I heard about your mum," says Becky, not coming in but passing me a plant with lots of bright yellow flowers. "I saw your sister in Morrisons and she told me."

"Oh, right," I say. I step to one side of the hallway to give Becky room to enter, but she doesn't move. "I just wanted to say that I hope she gets better soon," she says.

"Thanks," I say, putting the plant down on the hall cabinet. "She is already much better actually. She was ordering me around something crazy this morning – do the washing up, make the tea, build a conservatory!"

"Aww," says Becky smiling. "That's nice."

There is a pause.

"Um," I say. "I don't s'pose you want to come in? I've been working on a tattoo for my new band, Goat Fiend. You may have heard of us..."

"No, I'd better get going," says Becky, shaking her head. "Lots of History to do – Wars of the Roses."

"Oh, right," I say, "Flowers fighting! Ha!"

"Mmm. Well, see you then, Josh."

She turns and I say, "Um, Becky, I hope you won't mind me asking you this, but there is something I kinda need to know."

Becky shrugs. "OK."

"Are you a, um, lesbian?"

Becky blinks about three times. "No," she says.

"Oh, right."

"Why? Do you have a problem with lesbians?"

"No," I say. "God, no. It just might explain... Oh, nothing."

"Explain what?" asks Becky.

"I don't have a problem with lesbians at all," I say, backtracking. "I mean, one of my best friends is gay."

Becky is kinda staring now.

"He is!" I say. "Peter!"

"Yes, I know who you mean," she says.

I feel our conversation has taken a turn for the worse so I quickly try and change the subject.

"So, um, how are the boobs?"

11.30am: Inner Sanctum

How are the boobs?

How are the BOOBS!?

If I'd had several hours to think of the worst possible thing to say to Becky, I don't think I could've come up with anything better (i.e. worse!).

I pick Davey's piece of paper out of the bin and look through it.

```
Think before I speak! Will I regret what I
say later?
```

Um, yes.

```
For an easy conversation starter,
compliment their clothing.
```

Why didn't I do that? I thought she looked really nice with her cat ears.

```
...some things can be offensive. If in
doubt, DON'T RISK IT.
```

The only thing I have ever known Becky to take offence at is stuff about her boobs!

I open my wardrobe and stick Davey's sheet on the inside door. Obviously I need it way more than he does.

Tuesday 16th November

8.35am: Walking to college with Davey

"So are you cool having lessons with Ned?" I ask, passing Davey his drumming book. "He's all right, isn't he? And Lloyd. They're both very easy to get on with..."

"I left my sheet of rules there, didn't I?" says Davey. "It was in this book."

"Huh?" I say. "Sheet? Rules? What sheet of rules?"

"I have this list of things to help me in social situations," says Davey wearily. "You know, to stop me coming across as conversationally crap."

"Really," I say. "I never knew that."

Davey hoists his rucksack higher on his shoulder and sighs.

"Look, Davey," I say. "I *did* find your list but you honestly don't need to worry about that stuff. You are one of the nicest people I know."

"Yes, but being nice isn't enough. Girls don't like *nice*."

"Er, I think they do," I say. "*Everyone* likes nice."

Davey sniffs. "Oh, I don't know. Anyway, I've been thinking I probably get some of my anxiety problems from Mum. She can be a bit funny sometimes."

"Like what?" I ask.

"Well, we can only ever have yellow bubble bath because

it has to go with our yellow towels, yellow blinds and yellow bath mat."

"Sounds like OCD," I say.

"Obsessive compulsive disorder?"

"Obsessive *coordination* disorder."

Davey rolls his eyes and I give him a fist bump.

"Wait up, you two!"

We look round to see Peter legging it towards us, his coat flapping open.

"Have you finished with that pen, pencil and rubber you borrowed off me?" I say.

"Er, not quite," says Peter, leaning over and breathing heavily. "Sorry, I seem to have lost mine."

"Well, buy some new ones," I say.

"Will do," says Peter.

We start walking again.

"Hey, it's cold this morning, isn't it?" asks Peter. "I'm freezing and my throat's really sore. Can I borrow your scarf, Josh?"

I hand over my Children of Bodom scarf. "Do not lose it!" I warn him. "I had to save up for ages for that."

"I will treasure it," says Peter, smiling.

Wednesday 17th November

7.30am: Front room window

My mum and sister have just left for the hospital because Mum has to have a check-up to see if her stitches are dissolving OK. My sister's friend Darla came to collect them in her limited edition red Mini Cooper. My sister looked even more worried about the appointment than Mum did.

4.30pm: Kitchen

Mum is home and having a rest upstairs so I ask my sister how it went.

"OK," she says, "but I hate hospitals. Everyone looks ill."

"That's 'cause they *are* ill," I say.

"You think?" says my sister.

"Has Angus been in yet?" I ask.

"Angus?"

"Angus the tattooist."

"No," says my sister. "And I'd have thought you'd be more concerned about Mum than a silly tattoo."

This makes me mad for some reason so I say, "It's not a silly tattoo, and of course I'm concerned about Mum!"

"I don't know, Josh," mutters my sister, walking to the window and looking out. "You can be pretty selfish sometimes."

"*Me* selfish!" I say. "If anyone is selfish around here, it certainly isn't me!"

"Oh, so who is selfish then?" asks my sister, spinning round and staring at me, wild-eyed.

Usually I would back down here but today I am just too annoyed. "Well, you! D'uh!"

I squint my eyes and brace myself for the verbal equivalent of a level-ten tornado but my sister just turns back, saying, "Oh, calm down and eat some smoky bacon crisps. You're a right moody prick otherwise. And as for our tattoo deal?"

"Yes?"

"It's off!"

5.00pm: Inner Sanctum

Great. That's just great. I've a good mind to go and see Angus myself. I'm sure I could do his lashes for him. It can't be that hard if my useless, talentless loser of a sister can do it. And as for being moody without crisps? Well, that's just ridiculous. I can give up crisps just like that. The truth is, we've been out of crisps for three days now and it hasn't affected me one bit. I am *certainly* in no way moody.

5.15pm

I am finding it hard to concentrate on my differential calculus. I have come over sorta trembly and have a really bad headache.

6.35pm: Co-op Eight 'til Late shop

"Desperate, were you?" says Jackie the till operator as she scans my ripped-open family pack of smoky bacon crisps.

"Might have been," I tell her, mysteriously.

Jackie nods and gives me a knowing smile. "Help is out there," she says softly.

I look outside but I can't see anything but rain.

Thursday 18th November

1.00pm: Inner Sanctum

I am on the internet, researching addictions. I am both relieved and appalled to find out that there is indeed such a thing as crisp addiction. According to some people, crisps contain the ideal levels of salt and fat to make them *the* perfectly addictive food.

Plus, they have a chemical called monosodium glutamate which is kinda like speed for your mouth. Every time I eat crisps my taste buds get high!

However, all is not lost, as I have found a three-step addiction recovery programme that can apparently be adapted to suit all addictions:

1. Admit you have a problem.
2. Join a support group.
3. Reduce the harm.

OK, here goes...

"My name is Josh and I am a smoky bacon crisp addict," I say aloud. Step one done – it feels good!

I'm not sure about joining a support group, though. From my extensive experience (i.e. films), support groups tend to involve sitting in a circle in a draughty town hall listening to the problems of a load of strangers. There's a chance one of the strangers might be hot and desperate to have a crisp addict as a boyfriend, but it's quite small.

As for reducing harm, well, the idea here is that you do something similar but less harmful, e.g. smokers might use e-cigs or a nicotine patch. A patch releases a little of what you're addicted to into your skin and bloodstream. The problem with this is that crisp patches don't exist. Probably because all the crisp addicts out there are in denial.

Friday 19th November

4.20pm: Walking home from college with Davey and Peter

"In Biology I couldn't help noticing you had a crisp taped to your arm," says Davey.

"I know," I reply.

"There's no need to explain," says Peter.

"Isn't there?" says Davey, looking surprised.

"Josh is an addict," states Peter. "But it's OK, you're in a safe place, Josh, and with friends. No one here is gonna judge you."

"Right," says Davey, uncertainly. "Er, what is it you're addicted to exactly?"

"He's addicted to crisps," says Peter before I can open my mouth. "But that's no surprise when there's illness in the family."

"What?" I reply. "How do you...?"

"Becky," says Peter.

I'm about to say, "Jesus is nothing private any more?", when a knackered, metallic brown Escort screeches to a halt beside us blaring out 'Boogie 2Nite' by Booty Luv. (It pains me to admit I know this, but my sister plays it all the time.) The window is wound down and a round, smiling face appears.

"Wanna ride?" shouts Ollie.

"Jesus, Ollie," I say. "What are you doing? Have you passed your test?"

"Not... as such," says Ollie.

"Hmm, think I'll walk," says Peter. "Don't fancy gettin' in a car with a ridiculously over-confident, homicidal maniac. No offence."

Ollie rolls his eyes. "Ah, come on, live dangerously for once."

"I don't mind living dangerously," says Davey, "it's dying dangerously I don't like."

"Good point," I say.

"Will you ladies stop gabbing and get in," says Ollie. "Driving's easy. I could do it blindfolded."

"Yeah, well, please don't do that," I say, sighing and getting in the front beside him. "Promise me you'll *never* do that?"

"Hmm," says Ollie thoughtfully.

"And turn that off," I say. "I don't want that crap to be the soundtrack to my death, thank you very much. I want 'Not my Funeral' by Children of Bodom."

Ollie turns off the stereo and we leave the others to walk up the hill. As soon as I close the door, he floors the accelerator and I'm propelled back in my seat like an astronaut re-entering Earth's gravitational field.

"Damn it!" I say. "Can't you let me get my seat belt on?"

"Seat belt's busted," says Ollie cheerfully.

We roar up behind some poor person in a little Ford Ka and I grab the dashboard.

I am kicking myself for doing this. Why didn't I say no like the others? Why am I such a pushover? Anyway, the Ka has now sensibly turned off and we are caning it to the top of the hill. Suddenly I imagine the news on the BBC website:

Teen driver loses control as car swerves into path of articulated lorry

A 16-year-old boy was killed today as

the car he was travelling in was crushed beneath the front wheels of a lorry delivering vats of corrosive acid. The flattened and hideously burnt passenger was pronounced dead at the scene. Amazingly, the car's driver, who was reported as grinning madly right up to the point of impact, walked away from the vehicle unharmed.

The traffic lights on a pedestrian crossing up ahead turn red and I am very relieved to see Ollie applying the brakes and slowing.

"Right, well, thanks for that, Ollie," I say, as we draw to a slightly bumpy halt. "It's been a blast, but I think I'll get out and walk the..."

"Is that Wentworth?" says Ollie, suddenly.

I look up and see Wentworth beginning to cross in front of us.

"Jesus, yes," I say.

"Cool," says Ollie, laughing. "Shall I run him over?"

Ollie revs, the car belching clouds of smoke, and Wentworth looks round at us. He looks really small (even smaller than usual) and pretty scared.

"No, Ollie!" I cry, grabbing the wheel. "Don't do it!"

"Get off," says Ollie, pushing me away. "What the hell? I'm not really gonna run him over, am I?"

Wentworth hurries across, staring back at us when he gets to the other side. He then pokes out his tongue while giving me the finger.

"Damn it, Ollie," I say. "He was right there. You could've had 'im easy!"

Saturday 20th November

No band practice this weekend as Lloyd has family/church outings and Peter has a headache.

3.00pm: Inner Sanctum

After further internet research into addictions and related stuff, I find out that one in ten young people has some kind of mental health problem. One in ten seems quite a lot.

OK, so here's a quick rundown of some young people I know:

Davey – anxiety issues, panic attacks
Ollie – morning drinking, problems accepting responsibility, death wish
Becky – boob paranoia
Sister – sex maniac
Lloyd – energy drink addiction
Peter – interest in the occult, wild enthusiasm for leatherwear
(Obviously, neither of these are illnesses but they *are* weird.)
Me – crisp addiction
... and then there's Wentworth, of course – compulsive liar, control freak, psychopath.

Right, so according to my reckoning it's more like eight out of ten. Ozzy is my only friend that *doesn't* have some kind of issue.

And Ozzy is a ferret.

Sunday 21st November

11.15pm: Inner Sanctum

I'm about to start on my Biology homework when I realise I have left my textbook at college. This makes my crisp craving go off the scale.

11.35pm

It's no good. I'll have to eat the patch.

Monday 22nd November

8.30am: Inner Sanctum

I have now been living for three days without crisps, apart from the patch, that is. And that had lost its crispness and most of its smoky bacon flavouring so probably doesn't count.

My sister peeks in my room and says, "Oh my God. What will Mum say when she sees the state of this?"

I say, "Maddie, I get it. I need to make my bed, pick up my underwear, sweep up ten million of bits of sawdust, blah, blah. I'll do it, OK? You are nagging me more than Mum does!"

This is followed by another big row between me and my sister, which Mum probably heard.

My sister reminds me that Mum gets the results of her test this week and I am a being a selfish (her favourite word at the moment) dickhead.

8.45am: Walking to college

It's really cold today and my ears feel like two frozen fishcakes – which reminds me, Peter still has my Children of Bodom scarf. *And* he has my pen, pencil and ruler... God, he's got more of my stuff than I have!

I stop dead in the street.

You will need:

At least two items of clothing from the one you desire

At least three items in regular usage by the one you desire

Oh my God, the spell!

Wait, he only has one item of clothing! Phew.

Tuesday 23rd November

8.15am: Hallway

"Where's your beanie hat that Nan knitted you?" asks Mum as I'm about to head out the door.

"I'm not sure," I reply. "I think I must have left it... at... Ned's..."

OK, so if ever I needed a smoky bacon crisp it is now.

"I think Peter has it!" I burst out.

"Really," says Mum. "I thought that boy had more clothes than Victoria Beckham."

No, wait. I try to get a hold of myself. This is silly. It's just a coincidence that Peter borrowed my scarf. He had a sore throat. He'd forgotten his pencil case. It's all fine.

He fancies me! That's the only explanation. Two items of clothing for a spell to make me yearn for his love.

OK, so I can handle this. It's not good. Definitely not *ideal*, but I'll just have to take Peter to one side and gently explain...

Why has he done this? He's *knows* I'm not gay. He thinks he's God's gift to everyone, that's the trouble. What with his leathers and shades. God, I could kill for a crisp right now. And oxygen. I can't... breathe...

"Are you OK, Josh?" asks Mum, putting her hand on my shoulder.

"I'm fine," I mutter.

"Well, OK..." Mum starts to turn away.

"Mum!" I cry. "The worst thing possible has happened!"

Five minutes later: Lounge

Mum says that Peter knows I'm heterosexual and that the reason he borrowed those things was simply because he needed them – all perfectly normal and sensible. She also points out that the hat is most probably still at Ned's.

I feel a lot better and walk to college with a bit of a spring in my step.

5.45pm: Inner Sanctum

Good day at college today. Did quite well on my Biology test and the dinner lady gave me the biggest slice of pizza. Think she might fancy me. Shame she's older than my nan!

I get a text from Peter:

Hey, I seem to have your beanie! Sorry, must've picked it upwith my stuff. Will give it back to you along with your otherthings at college Thursday. xXPeterXx

My life is over.

Wednesday 24th November

1.00pm: Canteen with Ollie and Davey

Ollie puts down his knife and fork in the centre of his empty plate, leans back in his chair and pats his stomach. "That was disgusting," he says.

"Have you seen Peter?" I say.

"Nope," says Ollie. "He's gone to *le petit café dans le parc* for lunch with his dad."

"Is that the small French café that's in the park?" asks Davey.

"Dunno," says Ollie. "Hey, those girls over there are looking at us."

"What girls?" says Davey, loudly.

"That blonde one and her nerdy-looking friend," says Ollie, even louder.

"Shush, Ollie," I whisper.

"Mine's the blonde!" announces Ollie.

I can't believe I'm hearing this. "Ollie," I hiss, "you already have a girlfriend. Rose, remember?"

"Oh yeah," says Ollie.

Davey suddenly takes an intense interest in the napkin in his lap. "Uh-oh," he says. "They're coming over."

"Are you talking about us?" asks the blonde girl, giving Ollie a sub-zero stare.

"Maybe," says Ollie enigmatically.

"Only if you're, like, being disrespectful, then you should know I'm an expert in ju-jitsu and enjoy brutally torturing people who annoy me."

Ollie sits back in his chair and grins. "You can torture me any day, sweetheart!"

"Wow, he's either incredibly brave or incredibly stupid," says the nerdy-looking girl to her friend.

"Incredibly stupid," I say, under my breath.

4.20pm: Walking home with Davey and Ollie, eating reduced doughnuts

"Ow," says Ollie, tentatively moving his fingers where they were forced into a painful-looking ju-jitsu joint lock. "My hand hurts like hell."

"Shame," I say. "By the way, where's Peter?"

"What's the deal with you and Peter?" says Davey.

I stop dead in my tracks, which would have been dramatic had Ollie and Davey not kept on walking.

"Nothing," I say, running to catch up. "What would give you the impression that there's a..."(here I make the quotes symbol with my fingers) "...deal?"

"Er, well, you keep asking about him, that's all."

"Twice," I say. "I have asked about him twice!"

No one talks much for the rest of the walk home. We are each lost in our own private thoughts (and our doughnuts).

Thursday 25th November

8.40am: High street

On the way to college today, Davey says there's a guidance counsellor who is really nice and that I should go and see him.

"Look, I'm sorry I was such a dick yesterday," I say. "The last few days haven't been great for me mood-wise, but I'm fine now and I think I'm pretty much over the crisp thing."

Davey shrugs. "Just remember he's there. Every morning. You just have to email and make an appointment."

"OK," I say.

"He's good," persists Davey. "He's taught me to challenge my panicky thoughts – to take them to court kinda thing. Plus, he's shown me how to relax and breathe properly. It's helped."

I am glad for Davey, but I feel totally fine. I really don't need a counsellor.

12.20pm: Canteen

Ollie says, "Did you hear the joke about the girl who goes to the VD clinic? The doctor says, 'So, are you active sexually?' And she says, 'No, I just lie there!'"

We both crack up for about fifteen minutes.

Peter comes over with his tray of pizza and wedges and sits down. "Oh hey, Josh," he says reaching in his bag. "Here's your hat."

"Hmm," I say.

"And you're gonna be pleased because I've also got your pen and pencil."

Peter opens his pencil case and takes out my stuff. As he does this, I can't help but notice a black ribbon curled up inside.

You will need:
Some black ribbon...

"I didn't manage to get a new ruler yet," says Peter. "I don't suppose I could hold on to this one, just for this afternoon?"

"No you can't, Peter," I say. "And I may as well tell you right now that I am never gonna find you attractive. No matter how many freaky spells you cast or how many studded leather items you wear. I am not gay and even if I was I would go for someone with long hair and tattoos and stuff. But I'm not... so don't even bother growing your hair!"

"Huh?" says Peter. He looks genuinely dumbfounded.

"What's going on?" says Davey, who has now joined us with his lunch.

"Josh has had a breakdown," says Ollie. "It was only a matter of time."

"Peter knows what I'm talking about," I say. "He knows I saw his witchcraft book. There was a page marked in it about getting someone to fall in love with you. I can't believe..."

"Oh, oh," cries Peter, dropping his fork. "Oh no, Josh. That spell wasn't meant for *you*. I'm really sorry. I can see how you may have thought that but, oh my God!"

"Well, who's it for then?" I say, feeling less sure now.

Peter takes a deep breath. "It was for my parents. I thought I could make them get back together, maybe even love one another again. But it was no good. I met my dad yesterday for lunch at the French café in the park and he told me they're getting a divorce. He's moving out this weekend."

Friday 26th November

9.10am: Inner Sanctum

I can just about bring myself to go to college today.

First, Mum's just got her results and it wasn't good news. There were cancer cells in the sample they removed, so the cancer has spread. This means she's going to have to go in for another operation. Mum seems OK but my sister is pretty upset.

Second, I don't know how I'm gonna face Peter. I thought at the time he took it quite well, but I guess now he's had time to think about it he probably realises that I'm a complete and utter twonk, and that is why he hasn't responded to any of my grovelling texts.

In addition to the texts, I have tweeted my apologies, watered all his crops on his Facebook smallholding and washed everyone's hair in his BeautyVille salon. I have liked all his *Sims* walkthroughs on YouTube and commented that they are awesome and that Peter is a *Sims* genius. I have even posted an apology meme featuring the sad-eyed Puss in Boots character from *Shrek* on his Facebook wall. Social-media-wise, there is nothing more I can do.

12.40pm: Canteen with Ollie

I'm not feeling all that hungry but the canteen pizza does look really good today. It has loads of pineapple on it. Not only that, but they're serving my favourite dessert, apple pie and cream...

Three minutes later

"Peter," I say. "Don't bother queuing up. I've bought you lunch."

"But I didn't want pizza again," says Peter.

"Oh," I say.

"I'll eat it," says Davey, making a grab.

"No, you won't!" I say. "I haven't been a dick to you, at least not recently."

"It's OK," says Peter, taking the plate. "I guess you can't have too much pizza."

"Plus there's apple pie and squirty cream for afters!"

"Oh right. Jeez, I'm gonna be enormous at this rate."

"Did you get my texts?" I say, cautiously.

"No," says Peter. "I haven't had my phone on. I haven't even been on the computer since Dad told me about the divorce."

"Oh," I say.

There are so many things we could say to Peter, so many questions to ask. Like, where's your dad gonna go? Are you gonna live with him or your mum? What about your little brother? And most important of all: *are you OK?*

But none of us say anything. Instead we all sit silently, staring at the table while stuffing our faces.

After a while Peter says, "By the way, Josh, Wentworth got in trouble with Sean at Scouts last night. He threw a tantrum with some beanbags."

"Hmm," I say "Well, it's about time Sean realised what a dick Wentworth is."

Peter nods. "He's massively homophobic."

"I noticed," I say.

"And he bullies the younger Scouts, especially Tim."

"Yep, he's basically the kind of knobhead we could all do without."

Ollie lays down his fork and burps. "You could always put a spell on him," he suggests. "Like a really bad one."

7.00pm: Peter's Inner Sanctum

"Wow, how come you got all this stuff?" I ask.

We are looking in the bottom drawer of Peter's chest of drawers. I'm pretty sure it used to contain things like Pictionary, Dinosaur Snap and Junior Scrabble, but now it seems to be full of black candles, packets of dried herbs, engraved goblets and silver daggers. The smell of incense is enough to knock you unconscious.

"My mum bought most of it," says Peter, taking out a black cloth with funny symbols on. "She's a Wiccan."

"Is that someone who makes baskets?" says Davey.

Peter shakes his head. "It's a witch. One of the things that Dad got upset about was Mum moving over to the 'dark side'. He said it was symptomatic of a midlife crisis but Mum pointed out that at least she wasn't phoning sex lines and wearing jeans that were three sizes too small."

"Fair point," I say.

Davey looks at the candles suspiciously. "There aren't gonna be any Ouija boards, are there? Those things freak the hell out of me."

Peter smiles. "That's for summoning the dead. The only thing I know that's died is Julian's hamster and I don't know if Ouija boards work on them."

"Doubt it," says Ollie. "Hamsters can't spell."

"No, they're not the smartest of animals," agrees Davey.

Peter pulls out a little wooden table from under his desk and covers it with the black material.

"What's that for?" I ask.

"This is the cloth of mystic runes," says Peter darkly. "It's very important and, er, mystical." He lays the cloth out flat, and places three black candles on it, which he then lights with difficulty. The lighter he's using is a cracked one which he found on the pavement outside college.

"Right, Davey," he says, when all three candles are finally blazing away. "Please will you close the door and draw the curtains?"

Davey does so, while Peter rummages some more in the drawer. "Now, this," he says, holding up a little wooden figure in what looks like a Barbie dress, "is a genuine voodoo doll from the forests of deepest Zambia. We can communicate with this doll and it'll be like we're talking to Wentworth's spirit. We can ask the spirit to make Wentworth a nicer person, for example."

"Nah," says Ollie. "Talkin' won't work; you need to stick pins in it!"

I've gotta say, I'm inclined to agree with Ollie. Wentworth isn't the type to calmly listen to reason, and I very much doubt his spirit will be either.

"You sure?" says Peter. "I got to warn you that the spell we're about to cast is a very powerful one. It can only be used for *exceptionally* bad people."

"Yep, fine," I say.

"Once psychic contact is made," Peter goes on, "Wentworth will feel the full wrath of our fury. A multitude of evil spirits will be unleashed on his soul, causing nothing but suffering and an eternity of torment." As Peter announces this, a freak gust of wind moves the curtains and threatens to blow out the candles.

"Er, what was that?" asks Davey, looking round.

"Just the wind," says Ollie. "Come on, Peter, I'm meeting Rose outside Morrisons at eight."

We all sit cross-legged around the table of mystic runes with just the flickering candles for light. I am not sure if it's the sudden unexplained breeze or the thought of a multitude of evil spirits, but I am suddenly starting to feel uneasy.

"Is there anything we can do just to rough him up a bit?" I say. "I mean, we don't want to, like, kill him or anythin'!"

"That's true," says Peter. "But don't worry, I exaggerated with the eternity of torment bit. Basically he'll just feel a bit uncomfortable for a day or two. Well, depending on where we stick the pins, of course."

Davey has a sudden fit of the giggles and before long we are all cracking up.

"We can't put them *there*," I splutter.

"How about we just stick one in his arm?" Ollie says. "He can't die from that."

Peter nods and gives me a small piece of paper. "Right, Josh, I want you to write Wentworth's name in blood, six times."

"What?" I say.

"Write his name six times."

"Yes, I got that, but where am I gonna get blood?"

Peter grins and passes me a pin.

"Oh," I say. "Does it have to be mine?"

"I'm afraid so. Prick your finger or thumb on the side near the nail. Just give it a quick, sharp jab. It won't hurt at all."

"Fine," I say, stabbing away. "Ow! Liar!"

I have to stab myself about two hundred times to get any blood to appear but eventually there's enough to write the name six times. Trust Wentworth to have a really long name. Anyway,

Peter rolls up the paper, pulls off the doll's head and shoves the little tube down her neck. He then replaces the head and inserts a single pin into the doll's upper right arm.

"Now," he says. "We must chant a spell, three times over, increasing in volume with each verse. Let us link hands. Close your eyes and repeat each line slowly after me...

Demons and Angels!
By Gods and Goddesses
I curse thee, foul Wentworth
As punishment for hardships
Thy self has inflicted.
With this, mine blood,
I do curse thee:
With this black power
I do curse thee.

The wind once more whistles round the room, billowing in the curtains and rattling in the window frames. Somewhere a door creaks slowly open. Beside me, Davey is breathing heavily.

"Good," moans Peter, swaying slightly, his eyes still closed. "Now repeat again, but louder!"

Demons and Angels!
By Gods and Goddesses
I curse thee, foul Wentworth
As punishment for hardships
Thy self has inflicted.
With this, mine blood,

I do curse thee:
With this black power
I do curse thee!!

Outside, a dog howls at the moon. The wind is now so strong it extinguishes all three candles and we are left in utter darkness.

"Shit!" cries Davey.

"Do NOT break the circle," exclaims Peter, grabbing my hand forcibly. "Whatever happens, We *must* complete the chant..."

Demons and Angels!!!

"I gotta go," says Ollie, getting up. "Sorry, but Rose goes friggin' crazy if I'm late."

Saturday 27th November

4.15pm: Inner Sanctum

Massive crisp relapse! I got some money for taking Mrs Harris's orange poodle, Cindy Lou, out today and on the way back I stopped off at the Co-op and bought a giant multipack of smoky bacon crisps. I have eaten four packs in a row and now feel majorly depressed. I am depressed without crisps and I am depressed with crisps. I can't win.

Luckily, Ozzy is being very cute and crazy, jumping about on my duvet, so that cheers me up a bit.

Sunday 28th November

4.40pm: Inner Sanctum

We missed out on band practice again today as Peter has another sore throat! I hope he isn't like this when we are famous. People will get pretty pissed off if we have to keep cancelling our international tours.

Anyway, I spend most of the day in my Inner Sanctum on the computer. It's amazing, the stuff you can find on the internet. For example, I found out today that some dude in America has a house in the shape of a Gibson guitar. It took sixteen years to build and has six huge aluminium cables stretched across the roof for strings. Imagine tuning that!

I also learnt that no two people's farts smell the same and that the average chemical composition of a fart is:

59% nitrogen

21% hydrogen

9% carbon dioxide

7% methane

3% oxygen

and 1% stink (AKA hydrogen sulphide).

Why is it that the only chemistry I can remember is about farts?

Monday 29th November

8.30am: Kitchen

Mum has got the date for her surgery. It is 28th December.

"That's not too bad," I say. "It means you'll be home at Christmas!"

Mum smiles and says, "Yes, that's true."

"I wonder if the doctors dress up as Father Christmas on Christmas Day," I say. "Well, the male ones anyway. Although in these days of equality I guess the female ones might also want to.

There aren't really any traditional female characters associated with Christmas, are there? Apart from angels, I guess, though you can get male angels, like the Archangel Gabriel, for example..."

"Josh," says my sister, shaking her head. "Please shut up."

6.45pm: Inner Sanctum

I start to research some information about breast cancer on the internet but it's quite complicated and, besides, Mum is gonna be fine, so I don't need to know anything about it really.

Tuesday 30th November

6.10pm: Inner Sanctum

We got our target grades from college today. I am predicted:

Maths – B

Biology – C/D

English – B/C

Chemistry – E/F.

I remember one of my aims for the future was to pass an A level so I put half a tick next to aim number four in my leather-bound notebook.

I guess I might be able to go to university if I keep these grades up but I'm not sure I wanna go. I make a quick list of the pros and cons of going to university. I had been trying to give up making lists (aim number five) but giving up two addictions at once just isn't gonna happen. (I haven't touched a smoky bacon crisp since my massive relapse on Saturday, although I did nick a cheese and onion one off Davey in morning break.)

Pros:

1. Leave home!

2. Go to loads of parties

3. Meet loads of potential girlfriends who don't have boob issues

4. Get a degree (probably).

Cons:

1. Miss friends (kinda!) and Ned

2. Have to split up Goat Fiend

3. Miss Ozzy.

I'd like to take Ozzy but a) it's probably illegal; b) I don't think most university rooms are much bigger than his cage; and c) the smell may put some girls off. Which all means I'd have to leave him here to be looked after by Mum and Maddie – and I don't really think I can do that. I mean, I wouldn't trust Maddie to look after a cockroach. And they can survive nuclear fallout!

Wednesday 1st December

7.15am: Kitchen

Mum has left a couple of advent calendars on the counter: a Where's Wally knock-off for me called *Where's Willy* and a Hello Kitty knock-off for my sister called *Hiya Katty*. Today's chocolate is a blobby-looking tree. It tastes OK, though a bit chemically. My door has a snowman on the inside – traditional, but not very original.

12.45pm: College canteen

I have just found a seat when I notice Becky sitting on her own across the other side of the canteen. She looks a bit miserable so I make my way over with my tray. As I carefully negotiate all the chairs and tables I think back to Davey's rules on engaging brain before speaking. Whatever happens, I must not mention boobs or anything boob-related.

Becky looks up at me.

"Can I take a seat?" I ask.

"Suit yourself," she says, which is kinda encouraging, but not very.

"What you got?" I say, looking at her plate.

"Veggie burger. I'm a vegetarian now."

"Me too," I say.

Becky stares at my fish and chips.

"Except for fish," I say. "And the odd bit of chicken... and the very occasional burger, but I *never* eat pepperoni."

"I have the odd jelly baby," admits Becky.

"Mm-hmm," I say. Does Becky believe jelly babies are made out of real babies? Surely not.

"My mum isn't very good at catering to my vegetarian needs," Becky goes on. "She doesn't want to make two lots of meals. She says I'm being awkward."

"Well, that's crap!" I say, in a forceful voice that surprises both of us.

Becky clears her throat. "Um, well, she has a point, I guess."

"What I mean is that she should be more supportive," I go on. Unfortunately, as I say this, I feel my eyes drift down to Becky's chest. "As in moral support, I mean... not, er, physical..."

Becky blinks at me.

"Er, have you told your mum about Quorn?" I say. "I hear it's very versatile. Not to mention low in fat and easy to prepare."

"Yeah," says Becky. "But you know mums, they can be a bit set in their ways. How's *your* mum, by the way?"

"Not too bad," I say. "She has to go into hospital again, but it'll be OK. You know... it'll be fine."

"Well, give her my love," says Becky. She gathers up her things and smiles at me. "Thanks for the chat. I better go now. I have a History test this afternoon and I need to do some last-minute cramming."

"Sure," I say. "Breast of luck."

"Sorry?"

"*Best* of luck."

"Oh right, thanks."

Phew.

8.00pm

Hmm. Maybe I should be a vegetarian. I like animals and I like cheese, so it makes sense really.

Thursday 2nd December

Advent calendar – Chocolate is a sabre-toothed tiger (possibly meant to be a donkey). Inside door picture is bells joined by ribbon and holly.

7.15pm: Lounge

My sister is having a major binge session on TV, watching multiple episodes of *Come Dine with Me* back to back.

I'm still upset with her about the tattoo thing but I'm thinking that maybe if I make the effort to be extra nice she'll come round, eventually...

"Good episode?" I say.

"Yeah," says Maddie. "That blonde woman's fifty. She must've had a ton of Botox. Lower facelift too, probably."

"How can you tell?"

"Her lips seem a bit taut. And her nasal labial folds are almost non-existent."

"Oh right," I say, sitting down. "Interesting."

Maddie looks at me sharply but I just smile and try not to come across as creepy. (Peter once told me I have a creepy smile.) "She's gonna win though," says Maddie, looking back at the screen. "Everyone gave her a nine for her three-course Vegetarian Banquet."

"Her what?" I say.

"She did this vegetarian meal, with all these... "

"Brilliant!" I say. "Thanks, Maddie!"

"Huh?"

I leg it upstairs, grab my phone and start texting. I type quickly before I have a chance to talk myself out of it/see sense.

Text from me:

Becky, how d'you fancy coming over for a three-course vegetarian banquet cooked by me?

Thirty seconds later...

Text from Becky:

Love to XXX

Oh my God. I've just realised I have no idea how to cook a three-course vegetarian banquet!

But luckily I know a man who does.

Friday 3rd December

Advent calendar: Choc – old geezer (Santa?) / Picture – teddy bear

8.45am

Text from Peter:

Wentworth not at Scouts! Spell must've worked!

That'll teach him!

Saturday 4th December

Advent calendar: Choc – dwarf (elf?) / Picture – yellow cracker

4.50pm: Walking home from Ned's

Today at Ned's, we completed *'Paranoid'*. We can now play the whole thing from beginning to end with only around thirty duff notes. What's more, Ollie was wearing a black t-shirt with a skull on it. I knew the metal would get to him in the end; no one can resist its awesome lure for long!

Davey and me say goodbye to Peter, Lloyd and Ollie at the high street and carry on walking home together.

"Er, Davey," I say. "I've been thinking of doing a *Come Dine With Me*."

Davey's eyes light up like he's a dog hearing the word "walkies". "Awesome!" he says. "I'd love to come!"

"Er no, sorry. I mean with me and Becky. I'm hoping we can maybe get back together."

"Oh," says Davey.

"It's a kinda romantic, getting-back-together thing."

"You said that already."

"Right. So, er, can I run my menu past you?"

"Go on then," says Davey, sighing.

"I was thinking of doing vegetable soup to start," I say, "with croutons."

"OK," says Davey.

"Followed by cheese and tomato pizza with chips..."

Davey screws up his eyes as if in pain and waves me on.

"And, er, frozen peas," I say, less confidently. "Not that they'd be frozen. I'd cook them first!"

We've reached my house now and Davey follows me inside and up the stairs. "You haven't got much idea about entertaining, have you?" he says.

"What do you mean?" I say, slightly hurt.

"With a menu like that, you might as well skip the cooking and take her over to Greasy Al's Burger Bar on the A1."

"You heard me say croutons, right?" I tell him. "Croutons are posh."

"Croutons are stale bread," says Davey.

I take Ozzy out of his cage and lift him onto my lap.

"Fine," I say. "What do you suggest then, *Nigella*?"

Davey grabs some paper and pens from my desk and starts

writing out a menu. He does it really neat with slanty letters, swirls and everything. I think he must've been a girl in a previous life.

Davey's menu

Aperitif:

Olives, crudités, rosemary houmous

Starter:

Herby bruschetta with vine-ripened tomatoes and buffalo milk ricotta

Main:

Creamy pea and mint risotto with toasted brie, served with a charred leek and toasted walnut salad

Dessert:

Rich chocolate roulade served with fresh raspberries

I have to give Davey his due. He knows his stuff, food-wise.

"This sounds amazing!" I say, reading down. "But where am I gonna get buffalo milk ricotta and rosemary hummus?"

"*Hoo* moose," says Davey. "It's pronounced *hoo*moose."

"Rosemary *boomoose* then!" Davey's a bit of a food pronunciation Nazi, but I have to put up with it if I'm gonna get his help.

"I'll bring the ricotta from home," he says. "Everything else you should be able to make from scratch. I'll write out what you have to do."

"Umm, *Davey*," I say in a weedy voice "I'm not actually very good at following recipes..."

"When's the meal?" says Davey, folding his arms.

"7.30, Tuesday."

"Luckily for you, I happen to be free."

Sunday 5th December

Advent calendar: Choc – eagle (robin?) / Picture – yellow star

9.30pm: Lounge

My mum and sister are watching *Fight Club* with Brad Pitt. That is, Brad Pitt is in the film, not sat in our lounge. If Brad Pitt was sat in our lounge, there's no way he'd be able to watch anything because my sister would be snogging his face off.

"I'm thinking of cooking a vegetarian meal for Becky on Tuesday," I say. "Is that OK?"

"Mm-hmm," says Mum, her eyes stuck to the screen like iron filings on a magnet.

I watch the TV with them for a while until the scene where Brad rips off his top and flexes his annoyingly impressive muscles.

"Can I borrow a tenner from your purse for ingredients?"

"Yes, yes, whatever you like."

Nice one, Brad!

Monday 6th December

Advent calendar: Choc – eagle (robin?) / Picture – yellow star. Wait, wasn't that yesterday?

4.45pm: Shopping with Davey on the way back from college

Davey is chucking stuff in my basket like I'm someone who has money. "Davey," I say, "can't we get things from the cheap range? I can't afford all this high-quality stuff."

"We can't do this with inferior ingredients," says Davey. "If you want my help, you're gonna have to get the best."

"But I only have a tenner!"

"Fine," says Davey. "Put back the Bulgarian home-grown walnuts. It won't be the same without them, though."

Tuesday 7th December

Advent calendar: Choc – bomb (Christmas pudding?) / Picture – pair of testicles joined by ribbons (baubles?)

4.30pm: Kitchen with Davey

My mum and sister are going round my nan's so that me and Davey can have the kitchen to ourselves.

"See you later then," says Mum. "Can you make sure you wash everything up, Josh?"

"'Course," I reply.

"Is your mum feeling OK?" says Davey, after they've gone.

"She gets tired," I say. "But, yeah, I think so. She's got her operation soon."

I watch Davey trying to think of something to say and failing so I rub my hands together, all businesslike, and suggest we get started.

Davey has me preparing the chocolate roulade as this is the thing I'm least likely to screw up, apparently.

"Break the chocolate into chunks," commands Davey. "Use the rolling pin."

I whack the chocolate with the rolling pin and bits of it go flying off in all directions, mostly landing in the sink and under the fridge.

"Whoops," I say, bending down to pick a bit up.

"You aren't gonna use that?" says Davey.

"Sure," I say. "Haven't you heard of the five-second rule?"

"Huh?"

"If you pick something up within five seconds, it doesn't get germs on it."

"You're just saying that."

"Nope," I say. "It's been scientifically proven. I saw it on YouTube."

"Hmm," says Davey. "Becky isn't gonna want to get back with you if you give her food poisoning."

Davey is so negative sometimes.

7.27pm

Becky is due in three minutes.

"Davey," I say, "You have to go!"

"Are you sure I can't stay?" says Davey, undressing the chocolate roulade with his eyes. "There's easily enough for three."

I start pushing Davey into the lounge. "I'll do you a doggy bag. Sorry, but you're gonna have to go out the back."

"Huh?" says Davey, digging his heels in.

"She'll see you otherwise! If you climb over the back fence you'll be in Martin Street."

Ding dong.

"*Quick!*" I hiss, giving Davey a shove.

"Climb the *what*? Josh, can't I just..."

With a supreme effort, I propel Davey through the patio doors, slam the lounge door and run back down the hall to let Becky in. Typical. The one time I'd have liked her to be late and she's one minute early!

7.40pm: *Come Dine With Me* avec Becky

"Kids are mean," says Becky, nibbling her bruschetta. "Do you know I was ostracised all through middle school because I couldn't do a cartwheel?"

"A cartwheel?" I ask.

"If you couldn't do a decent cartwheel you were nothing at my school. Nothing."

"Jeez," I say.

"I bet you could do great cartwheels," says Becky, smiling and leaning forward to touch my knee.

"Um," I say. "I can't actually remember. My forward rolls were quite good, I think."

"My forward rolls were crap," says Becky, leaning back again.

"Oh dear," I say. "Um, do you like the *hoo*moose?"

"*Hoomoose*? Oh, you mean *hummus*. Yeah, I love it. I really like what you've done with the seasoning."

"That's the rosemary," I say. "It's a vegetable. No, wait, I mean herb."

"Right," says Becky. "Are you *sure* you didn't get any help?"

"Yes," I say. Becky looks like she expects me to say more but I have learnt my lesson regarding lying – keep it simple and do not elaborate.

"Well, you've done very well," she says finally.

"Ready for the pea risotto?" I say.

"I'm ready for whatever you want to give me!" says Becky, licking her lips in slow motion and tossing back her hair.

"Er, risotto is kind of it," I say, getting up to take her plate. "Sorry, we don't have much else in the house. Is that OK?"

"That's fine," says Becky, although she sounds a bit disappointed. Maybe she's not a big fan of rice.

Wednesday 8th December

Advent calendar: Choc – bin lorry (sleigh?) / Picture – yellow square (present?)

1.30pm: Inner Sanctum

We have our mocks next week and I am just about to start revising when I get a text from Becky inviting me shopping. I have to be honest, there are about a billion things I would rather be doing with Becky than shopping (including revising and shaving my eyeballs), but if I want to get back with her I have to look keen and show willing. So I text back and say:

Yes, great. I really love shopping and I really like you so that will be doubly brilliant!

1.50pm

On reflection, I may have overdone that a bit.

5.30pm: Inner Sanctum, exhausted

Why do women love shopping so much? Becky already has lots of jeans. I know this because I've seen them in her wardrobe and yet we spent 1 hour 45 minutes examining jeans today. If I have to look at another copper rivet, I may go insane.

On the plus side, Becky let me hold a couple of her fingers on our way back to the bus station.

Thursday 9th December

Advent calendar: Choc – nothing! Did I get the days wrong or has my thieving sister nicked my chocolate? / Picture – old sock (Xmas stocking)

9.40pm: Inner Sanctum

I am engrossed in a YouTube video of a boxer dog trying to eat a lime when there's a knock at the door. As usual, my sister refuses to get off her arse so I have to run down the stairs and get it.

Peter is standing there looking upset. "Wentworth wasn't at Scouts again," he says. "I'm worried, Josh."

I let Peter in and we go to my Inner Sanctum and collapse on the sacred resting place (bed).

"Have you asked his friends?" I ask.

"I don't think he has any."

"What about Sean?"

"Sean isn't really his friend."

"No, Peter, but have you asked Sean where he is?"

"What if he's dead?" cries Peter, ignoring this and grabbing me by the arm. "What if you've killed him?"

"*Me...* killed him?" I say, pushing Peter off. "You're the one who did it!"

"It was *your* blood!"

"It was *your* spell!"

Peter sighs and sits back. "I knew this was a bad idea," he says.

"Ollie always has crap ideas," I say.

"Yes," agrees Peter. "Bloody stupid Ollie. He never thinks things through... They'll suspect *us*, though. They know we didn't like him, especially you, when you tried to drown him in orange juice!"

"Shit!" I say.

"The police will be round in a few days," Peter goes on. "You mark my words. We have to get our story straight, Josh! What are we gonna do?"

"Well, for a start, you'll need to get rid of your witchcraft stuff," I say.

"Yes," says Peter, nodding.

"Everything. And don't just put it in the bin. They search bins."

"I'll bury it," says Peter. "I'll go out at midnight tonight and bury it in the woods at the back of the park."

"That's good," I say. "Make sure you wipe any fingerprints off and wear gloves."

"Right," says Peter. "Oh God, I'm not cut out for this CSI stuff. I'm not good at staying one step ahead of the law. Plus, I just know I'll crack under interrogation."

"Whatever happens," I say, "you must *not* crack under interrogation. If you do, *all* our lives will be finished."

Peter looks miserable. "Will you come with me tonight, Josh? *Please?*"

11.50pm: Outside Peter's house

Peter emerges silently from the back of his house dressed all in black, including a black stocking on his face and holding a bulging black bin bag.

"Hi," he whispers.

"You got it all?" I say.

"Yes, let's go."

We get all the way to the top of his road before we are stopped by the police...

11.59pm: Peter's house

"I really am so sorry to have bothered you with this," says Peter's mum. "I am in the middle of a divorce and it seems to have had an unsettling effect on my son."

"Not a problem," laughs Sergeant Clegg. "I gotta say, this has made my night! I can just imagine the two of them up there prancing around in the park, casting spells." He ruffles Peter's hair. "Save it for Halloween, eh, boys?"

"Ha ha, yes. Will do," says Peter, nervously.

Sergeant Clegg lets himself out, still chuckling, and we are left in the lounge with Peter's mum, who is definitely *not* chuckling.

"Er, maybe I should be getting home," I say.

"Yes, I think you should," she says.

Friday 10th December

Advent calendar: Chocs – dwarf, hyena, bomb, bauble, blob tree, hyena, bell, bell / Pictures – yellow things. I have eaten all my chocolates up 'til 18th December.

10.45am: College grounds, sat on bench

"Was your mum really mad?" I say.

"Not *really* mad," says Peter. "But then I didn't come clean about Wentworth. I said I wanted to bury it all because it was freaking me out, which is basically true if you think about it. She thinks it's 'cause of Dad leaving."

"Handy," I say.

"Yeah, seems divorces are good for something after all."

There's a bit of a heavy silence here, but then I say, "I guess we *were* kinda over-reacting. Maybe we should give it one more week."

"Actually," says Peter, getting up to go back in, "it's the Scouts Christmas meal/Laser Quest outing on Monday night. *Everyone* goes to that."

This is true. The Christmas meal is the highlight of our Scouting calendar, especially as Sean gives out a load of badges and Haribo.

"Right," I say, "let's see what happens on Monday then."

10.15pm: Walking Becky home

Becky came over to revise with me this evening. She is very committed. To be honest, I may as well have been revising on my own for all the social interaction we had.

"Will I see you over the weekend?" I ask, when we get to her house.

"I'm not sure. I'll probably be revising," she says.

"Can I have a hug then?"

"Just a quick one," says Becky.

We embrace and I pucker up my lips and lean forward to give her a kiss, but she has already turned and is halfway up her drive. Did she expect another three-course meal this evening? I can't keep that up forever.

Saturday 11th December

1.00pm: Ye olde belfry (Loft)

Mum says we can get the stuff down for Christmas, which should be exciting but isn't because our loft ladder is basically evil. One time, it shot out of the hatch, almost slicing my arm off. Another time, after I had carefully slid each section together and locked them in place, it sprang back up into the loft, nearly giving me a cheap but very unflattering facelift.

Anyway, I manage to get the ladder down and ascend to the loft without incident. I used to try and imagine this as a special place full of dark and intriguing secrets, but the only thing our loft is full of is mouldy baby clothes, cobwebs and something that looks like orange candyfloss (insulation).

"Don't tread between the beams!" yells Mum from the landing.

"You'll come straight through the ceiling."

Mum says this every year. If I am living at home when I'm fifty, she will still be saying this.

Ten minutes later, after pulling a load of musty boxes down on my head, we are in the lounge rooting through reams of sad, moulting tinsel and tacky baubles. My sister puts the artificial tree up and starts yanking out the branches. It looks like the trees you see in Geography textbooks showing the destructive effects of acid rain. Meanwhile, I am looking for something important. I am searching for the snowman decoration I made out of a washing-up bottle and loads of cotton wool back when I was in infant school. My snowman was the best in the class. The teacher said so. She said, and I remember this all these years later, that it had *attitude*. I didn't know what that meant at the time but I knew it was good.

"Er, where's Mr Snowy?" I ask Mum.

Mum looks at my sister. "Oh," she says. "Oh, he'll be in there somewhere."

I keep looking. I find my sister's squashed toilet roll angel and she grabs it gleefully and puts it on the top of the tree, but I still can't find Mr Snowy.

"Maybe it was in another box that's still in the loft," says my sister.

"Yes, that'll be it," says Mum. "We'll bring him down next year. Give him this Christmas off."

"He doesn't want this Christmas off!" I cry. "This is his only chance to shine. He's in that loft eleven-twelfths of the year!"

Irritated, I storm back upstairs, climb into the loft and search around some more, but there are no other Christmas boxes. As I come back down the ladder I hear Mum and my sister talking. "I must've chucked it out last year. It was covered in mould..."

"Shush...he's coming..."

Mum and my sister give me freakishly big smiles as I go into the lounge, but my sister soon loses hers when I grab the angel off the tree and run with it into the kitchen.

"No, no," she cries, chasing after me. "Please, Josh. Please don't hurt Gabriella..."

I throw the angel back into the lounge and scowl at them both.

"There's some crisps in the kitchen cupboard," says Mum.

"Mum, you can't just buy me off with crisps," I say. "Good God, you have hurt my feelings! I now expect a far better present this year because of this betrayal of my trust. Um, which kitchen cupboard?"

Sunday 12th December

4.30pm: Ned's

I am happy though exhausted today because after three hours of blood, sweat and almost continuous swearing we can nearly play 'Bed of Razorz' by Children of Bodom!

Luckily me and Lloyd already knew it quite well. The others, though, rose heroically to the challenge and, it has to be said, I am proud of them. Peter hasn't quite got the same growl as Alexi from Children of Bodom but he's almost there.

"Cool," croaks Peter, when we have finally decided to call it a day. "Now, before we go, I want you to close your eyes and take a piece of paper out of my hat."

"Why?" asks Lloyd.

"Secret Santa!" squeaks Peter. His voice really has gone weird.

"Do we have to?" I say. "I haven't got much money and last year Ollie gave me a half-eaten sandwich."

"Sorry," says Ollie. "I forgot we were doing it. Besides, that was my lunch. Only a true friend would give up his lunch for his mate."

"Fine," I say. "But can we put a limit of £5 on it?"

The others nod.

Ollie goes first and starts laughing hysterically when he looks at his piece of paper. Great, he's got me again. This time I'll probably get half a sausage roll.

I have Davey, which is OK, although Davey pretty much has everything already.

Monday 13th December – mocks

9.15am: Inner Sanctum

It's mocks all this week. The idea is to try and prepare us for the real thing when we go back after the Xmas holidays. I'm pretty worried though because A levels are really hard. They're, like, really *advanced*.

Text from Peter:

Good news – came 31st out of 36 on Laser Quest. My best score eva. Bad news – no Wentworth!

1.00pm: College gym, sitting Biology mock

Biology mock is fiendishly difficult and it doesn't help that I have

Wentworth now to add to the list of worries crashing round in my head. Why am I so worried about Wentworth? FFS!

Tuesday 14th December

9.00am: College gym, sitting Chemistry mock

Hmm, turns out the Biology mock was quite easy. At least compared to the Chemistry mock! I look at the next question:

> **Q5. Draw a diagram to show how two molecules of hydrogen fluoride are attracted to each other by intermolecular forces. Include all partial charges and all lone pairs of electrons in your diagram.**

I draw:

Somehow, I don't think this will get me many marks.

1.20pm: College library, on computer

"What's his surname?" asks Ollie, logging into Facebook.

"I dunno," I say.

"Well, there can't be many Wentworths," Ollie goes on. "I'll type that in and see what we get."

"There he is!" I say, jabbing my finger at the screen.

"Yeah, that's him all right," says Peter. "The poser!"

While it's true that Wentworth's selfie does show him wearing shades, Peter's a fine one to talk about posing on Facebook. In his pic, he's wearing a rhinestone-encrusted leather vest!

Anyway, we have a problem in that Wentworth has set his privacy settings to max. According to his page, Wentworth only shares information with his friends.

"I guess the only other option is to go round his house," says Peter, "except none of us knows where he lives."

"I do," I say.

Everyone looks at me.

OK, so I gotta admit it's weird (and slightly worrying) that I can remember Wentworth's address. I am crap at remembering things to do with my A levels and yet I can recall, almost word for word, Wentworth begging me to go round and finish that stupid Monopoly game at his house:

"I only live round the corner, 24 Wilton Avenue. We'd be there in five minutes."

"It's 24 Wilton Avenue," I say. "Don't ask me how I know."

"Well... the thing is..." says Peter, suddenly stalling, "even if we *did* go round his house, what would we say? We can't just knock on the door and go 'Hi, just checking you're still breathing. We thought we might have accidentally/on purpose killed you.'"

"Yes, but what if he becomes violent?" says Davey. "You said yourself he's a psycho."

"Nah," I say. "Wentworth is a major jerk but he's not a knife-wielding, meth-addicted maniac. At least, he wasn't when I saw him last."

"Hmm," says Davey, not convinced.

"Well, I'm going anyway," I say. "I need to find out what's happened to him. What I'd really like from you three is loyalty, honour and a beating heart!* Who's with me?"

The silence is deafening. I watch dust settle on the computer screen. Outside, a few remaining leaves drift down gently from the trees.

"Oh, me, I s'pose," says Peter eventually.

"Yeah, yeah," says Ollie.

"Fine," says Davey. "But if I have a panic attack, it'll be your fault."

"Cool," I say. "Oh, and I don't think we'll need to knock on his door. We can just wander by and see if there's any activity going on. If we go about teatime they'll probably be sat in their kitchen eating. All we need to do is get a glimpse of him looking fairly healthy, with like all his limbs and stuff, and then we can be off."

The others nod.

"Let's meet outside the Scout hall at 7pm," I say. "Oh, and Peter?"

"Yeah?"

"*Don't* wear tights on your face."

7.00pm: Scout hall

Peter is not wearing tights on his face. So that's good. What isn't so good is that Ollie has brought Bongo.

"I know," says Ollie, seeing my face, "but Mum insisted. He hasn't had a walk today."

"Also, he might be good if there's any trouble," says Davey.

I look down at Bongo's broad, honest and dopey face. He'd

*As said by the mighty Thorin Oakenshield in The Hobbit when he is recruiting volunteers to slay the mighty dragon.

be about as much use in a fight as a daddy-long-legs, but I give him a pat and say, "OK. Let's go."

We wander down Wilton Avenue looking at the numbers either side. The houses are 1940s semis with small front gardens and drives. We get to number 24, which looks kinda crappy. There's an overgrown hedge separating the garden from the pavement, a fridge lurking in the grass (like a jagged tooth) and a decaying caravan on a pile of bricks. They've made a brilliant effort with the Christmas lights though. There's even an inflatable snowman on the roof. Nice one!

Unfortunately, apart from the fairy lights, the front of the house is in darkness.

"Damn," I say. "We're either gonna have to knock on the door and ask to see Wentworth... or creep round the back."

"No way," says Davey, shaking his head. "That's trespassing!"

"Ssh," says Ollie. "Someone's coming."

While we were talking, a light behind the front door has come on, and as we look, the door opens and two girls come spilling out, giggling.

"Let's move up here a bit," whispers Ollie, starting to walk up the street. The others follow but something makes me stay.

I creep closer and back silently into the hedge while they pause on the front path.

They are kissing now: big, noisy, smacking kisses – which is quite interesting as it's not something you see every day. But then one of the girls pulls herself away and I catch my breath and stagger a bit. Oh my God!

Becky looks up and screams.

"It's OK," I say, waving my hands and coming out of the bush.

"It's me."

"Josh?" says Becky. "Josh, is that you?"

"What's goin' on?" says a great bear of a man, appearing in the doorway. This guy is about six foot six, has a vest covered in what looks like tomato sauce (blood?), and arms the size of elephant legs!

"That creep was watching us!" cries a girl I assume to be his daughter. "The pervert!"

"It's OK," says Becky, waving her hands. "I know him."

But the Bear isn't listening to Becky, and before I can get my shit together, both my feet have left the ground and I'm suddenly being shoved up hard against the rusty caravan by my collar.

"What the hell you doin' in my garden?" growls the bear.

"He was spying," says the girl, who I am starting to dislike more and more. "Get off seeing two girls kiss, do yer? Wanker!"

"No, no, he's not like that," says Becky.

"No, I'm not," I say, shaking my head. "I'm totally not a lesbian-obsessed pervert!"

The Bear glares at me and tightens his grip.

"What you gonna do with 'im, Dad?" says the girl. "You gonna duff 'im up a bit?"

I shake my head again and make a sad face.

"You two get off," says the man. "You'll be late for your film. Leave me to sort this out."

"Er," says Becky, "please don't hurt him," but the other girl tugs hard on her arm and she lets herself be dragged away.

"So you wanna tell me what's goin' on?" growls the Bear.

For some reason, possibly because his hand is now around my neck and pushing hard on my vocal cords, I have lost the power of speech. "I... uh..."

The bearlike one sighs and starts to drag me into the house when I hear Ollie shouting. "Oi, arseface! Leave 'im alone!"

Way to go, Ollie: enrage him even more.

Then Bongo suddenly remembers he's a dog and starts barking frantically and straining at the leash.

"Get 'im!" yells Davey, as Ollie lets Bongo off. "Attack, Bongo! Bite him on the dick!"

Bongo races up to the guy, and for a minute I think he really *is* gonna attack but then he starts wagging his tail and licking the guy's crotch.

"Geroff, stupid mutt," roars the Bear. He manages to shove the overly affectionate Bongo out of the way with his knee before looking back at me. "Right, you, one last chance to tell me what you were doin' or I'm callin' the police."

"He's here to see me," says a small voice from out of nowhere. "He's my friend."

I look up to see Wentworth standing in the doorway.

7:25pm: Wentworth's Inner Sanctum with Davey, Peter, Ollie, Bongo and me

"Nice room," I lie, looking round.

"Thanks," says Wentworth. "Sorry there's only the bed to sit on."

"That's fine," we all say, sitting down on the crumpled duvet (Lego *Star Wars*).

"Thanks for helping out back there," I say.

"S'OK," says Wentworth. "Thanks for coming to see me!"

"Er, we didn't actually..."

"No problem," interrupts Peter. "We wondered why you hadn't been at Scouts."

"I was banned," says Wentworth.

"Banned?"

Wentworth nods. "Sean told me off for being violent. He made me see this counsellor guy about my anger issues."

"Right," I say. "So, what did you do with him?"

"We talked about my anger issues, genius!" yells Wentworth. "Oops, sorry. Sometimes I lapse a bit."

"S'OK," says Ollie. "It's good you're doin' somethin' about it."

"Yeah, really good," agrees Davey, shifting slightly nearer the door.

Wentworth looks at the carpet. "Thanks. And I'm, er, sorry for what I said about Becky, Josh."

"Well, turns out you were right," I say, remembering what had just happened outside.

Wentworth shrugs. "She's nice, though."

"Yeah," I say. "She is."

We talk for another ten minutes or so, but then Bongo starts gnawing on some of Wentworth's hand-painted soldiers, so we decide to make a move before he loses his temper again.

"Well, see you at Scouts one day, maybe?" says Peter, when we get down into the hall.

"Yeah," says Wentworth. "Cheers for coming over."

Wentworth raises his arm to wave goodbye and then grimaces.

"What's up?" I ask.

"Oh, nothing," he says. "I just sometimes get this really weird stabbing pain in my arm."

Wednesday 15th December

1.10pm: Inner Sanctum

I should be revising but instead I have spent a lot of today thinking about last night. I receive an apologetic text from Becky, saying that she's been very confused about her sexuality but that she's much happier now that she knows she's definitely a lesbian. "I do like you a lot," she says. "Just not in that way."

You and everyone else, I think, as I scribble out aim number 1 in my leather-bound notebook. Looking on the bright side, though, even if Becky is no longer my 'girlfriend', she is a friend who's a girl, so that's definitely progress.

Kinda.

Thursday 16th December

8.00am: Inner Sanctum

Mum is really tired today and doesn't go in to work. I wish she was having the operation now. It's not fair that she has to keep waiting. She gave me a leaflet a few days ago called 'So, your mum has cancer'. I don't need to read it, though, because she soon won't have cancer, so I just shove it to the back of my drawer.

I have a Maths mock this morning. I have revised and could do OK so I should definitely go, especially as it's my best subject. Trouble is, my mind is full of fragments of my dream. It wasn't a very nice dream. I'd had my head removed for some kind of horrible experiment. Someone in a hospital was trying to glue it back on but they were making a rubbish job of it and in the end they gave me up as a lost cause and went off to have their lunch. I hope the people who operate on Mum are more committed.

3.10pm: Inner Sanctum

I have been in my bedroom most of the day. I have eaten a lot of crisps. I lied to Mum and told her I didn't have college. I feel bad about not going but it's too late now. I just don't know if I can hack exams at the moment.

Ozzy lets me lift him up to see the stars. Orion's belt is very bright tonight – I can see all three stars sparkling, even though I have a street lamp right outside my window. I read on the internet that all sorts of creatures have been sent into space: mice, geckos, even fish. God knows how much water slopped out of their tank on take-off!

I get sad when I think about the monkeys they send up, though, and the little dog, Laika. She must've been so scared and alone. After Laika died she circled the Earth over two thousand times before the rocket she was in burnt up in the Earth's atmosphere. She did something amazing – going into space, but all she wanted was to be someone's pet and go down the park and sit in front of the fire or on a lap somewhere.

I don't know why people have to be so horrible to other people and to animals. There's enough suffering in this world that can't be avoided, without creating more.

Friday 17th December

9.10am: Room 4ED

I should be in the gym sitting my English mock but instead I am in Room 4ED talking to Alex, the college counsellor. I realised Davey was right and that I *do* need someone to talk to about stuff.

"So you say you've been eating a lot of crisps?" says Alex.

I nod.

"You know smoky bacon crisp addiction isn't *really* a thing, don't you?" says Alex.

"Isn't it?" I say.

Alex tilts his hand up and down. "Not really, I don't think."

"I guess the crisps were just something... something to help take my mind off things."

Alex nods. "You wanna tell me about it?"

10.10am

I have told Alex about it. I have told him so much about it and everything else in my life that the poor guy probably wishes he'd never asked!

I told him about Becky and her girlfriend and that I'm worried I won't find someone who likes me.

I told him I'm worried I will never fulfil my dream of becoming a death metal guitarist.

I told him I'm worried about all the animals you hear about on Facebook that are being cruelly treated, and about starving foxes and dogs dying in space.

I told him I'm worried about screwing up my exams and not

getting into university.

And then I took a really deep breath and told him I'm worried about Mum not being able to beat cancer.

Alex listens and nods and listens some more.

Saturday 18th December

10.10am: Inner Sanctum

I have read the cancer booklet Mum gave me and am now on the internet following up some of the links on the back of it. Alex told me I should find out as much as possible. He said information is power and knowing what we have to deal with will make me feel more in control. I think he's right.

Sunday 19th December

Advent calendar: I finish my advent calendar, including the special large chocolate for 24th December that says *Merry Christmas!* or, in my calendar's case, *Mary Chrismast!!!* The spelling leaves a bit to be desired, but the chocolate tastes OK.

8.00pm: Walking home from Ned's

We stayed quite late at Ned's today fine-tuning 'Bed of Razorz' and working on our fourth song. Which is, wait for it – 'The Final Countdown' by Europe. OK, so it's not exactly death metal, but it's easy to play and will give Ollie something to get his teeth into as it has some good keyboards.

We are just approaching the high street when Peter says, "Ah, it's no good, I can't hold it in any longer."

"Hold what in?" asks Davey.

"OK, brace yourselves," says Peter, stopping dead. He turns to face us. "You know how we never have anywhere to go on New Year's Eve because we are generally unpopular and most people hate us?"

"Yes," I say.

"Well, not any more, because, get this, my dad's gonna be round his girlfriend's place on New Year's and he said I can have a party round his flat!"

"That's cool, Peter," I say, "but it'll be a pretty crap party if it's just us there, won't it? No offence, guys."

"Ah, but I have thought of that," says Peter, "and I have come up with a plan to make sure that this is the best party ever!"

"What's that?" says Davey. "Are you getting loads of food in?"

"I am," says Peter, "but that's not it."

We start walking again and cross the high street at the lights.

"Loadsa booze?" asks Ollie.

"Certainly, yes."

"Energy drinks?" suggests Lloyd.

"If you want them, sure," says Peter. "Any more guesses?"

"Oh just tell us, Peter!" exclaims Davey. "No, wait... Balloons?"

"Nope."

"Just tell us," I say.

Peter grins. "I'm hiring a band!"

"Wow," I am impressed. "That must be costing a lot."

"Not really," says Peter. "They said they'd do it for free."

"What?" says Ollie. "Who are these suckers?"

Peter starts giggling. "Us!"

Five minutes later, on bench in park

"Peter, there's no way we can do it," I say for the six-millionth time. "No way!"

"You are such a doom merchant," says Peter. "You are the Penguin of Dooooooooom!"

"No, I'm not," I say. "I just know a bad idea when I see one."

"Why is it a bad idea, then?" asks Peter.

I take a deep breath. "Well, first of all we only know three and a quarter songs. And second of all, WE SUCK!"

"Would've been cool, though," says Ollie.

Monday 20th December

4.30pm: College corridors

I should be going home, but I have to walk the corridors of our college ripping the posters Peter's designed for his party and our band's first ever gig off the notice boards.

I cannot believe he has done this! We are nowhere near ready for mass exposure. Nowhere near!

"Hey, can I see that?" says a hipster girl, holding out her hand.

"Um, well, OK," I say.

"Hmm, this looks all right," she says, reading the sheet I've just ripped down.

I gotta admit, the posters do seem quite well designed, although I could've done them better. The Goat Fiend logo is far too readable, for example.

"Goat Fiend. Haven't heard of them but I like some metal," the girl goes on. "Plus, me and my mates were wondering what to do for New Year's. Why are you taking it down? Is it cancelled?"

"Er," I hestiate.

"Only it looks pretty awesome."

And then, because she is nice and I can't help myself, I say, "Nah, it's not cancelled, just kinda full, but I'm sure we can fit a few more in. See you there, maybe?"

She nods, takes the leaflet and leaves.

Oh God!

Tuesday 21st December

2.15pm: Break up from college. Morrisons car park with Ollie, Davey, Lloyd and Peter.

College is over for a week or two and we are celebrating by doing the Secret Santa thing.

"Wow, it's really big," I say. "I'm jealous."

Peter enthusiastically pulls the wrapping paper off his very large present to reveal...

...a toy ironing board.

"It's a toy ironing board," says Peter, his face taking on a slightly twitchy expression.

"Cool. My turn!" cries Ollie.

Ollie has received a packet of novelty bath salts that have *Finest Quality Crystal Meth! NOT FOR HUMAN CONSUMPTION!* printed on the label. "Awesome," he says. "I can plant some of these round my room. Mum'll go mental!"

I think I catch Lloyd grin, so obviously these are from him. I have bought Davey a metronome. I hope he doesn't find it too offensive. I wait anxiously as he opens it.

"Wow," says Davey. "It's a... a... What is it, actually?"

"It's a metronome," I say. "I hope you don't mind, Davey. All good drummers should have a metronome. It doesn't mean you're crap or anything."

"So *you* bought it for me," says Davey, smiling and setting the metronome swinging.

"Damn!" I say.

"Well, thanks," says Davey. "I love it. Tick tock, tick tock... ha ha."

I open my present and find a mug with the words *KEEP CALM AND TICKLE A FERRET* on, which is very cute, although if you tickled most ferrets you'd end up in the emergency department of your nearest hospital. Meanwhile, Lloyd is happily unwrapping his gift, which turns out to be... a giant chocolate dick. Original!

We say our goodbyes and agree to meet up at Ned's tomorrow for a desperately needed rehearsal. I am just about to cross at the lights, when I notice Lloyd running back towards me, so I stop to let him catch up.

"I just wanted you to know, I've been praying for your mum," he says breathlessly. "Actually, our whole church has. My mum led a prayer for her last Sunday."

"Really?" I say.

"I hope you don't mind," he says.

"No, of course not."

Lloyd nods. "OK. Gotta go, that's my mum now."

I see Lloyd's mum turn into the top of the car park in her silver Nissan. She waves at me and smiles as Lloyd jogs over.

"Uh, Lloyd," I shout.

"Yeah?" he says, looking back.

"Thank you. And thank your mum too."

Lloyd raises a hand and gets in the car.

Wednesday 22nd December

4.25pm: Rehearsal round Ned's

I have calculated that we probably have five sessions, maximum, before our New Year's gig. Is this enough to avoid a huge and highly humiliating train wreck? I very much doubt it, but at least 'The Final Countdown' is coming along so we may have four songs to play!

"You'll be fine," says Ned, sensing our anxiety as we pack up our stuff. "When I was playing in Atomic Dwarf, we had some truly terrible gigs. Once or twice I thought we'd never be able to set foot outside our homes again, but drunk people have short memories."

I'm not sure if this is encouraging or not so I just nod.

"It'll be pretty embarrassing if we get booed," says Davey.

"Or bottled," adds Ollie.

"Or threatened with knives," I say, instantly regretting it.

"I think we need an audience," announces Lloyd. "We haven't practised in front of anyone apart from Ned. If we let a few other people see us, we'll feel a lot more confident."

Hmm, I wonder who we can get to be in an audience...

Thursday 23rd December

7.30pm: Ned's

"Come on then," says my sister. "We need to get to Tiger Tiger soon for the half-price cocktails."

My sister and Darla are squashed up against the bay window in Ned's front room. They are both dressed for a night's clubbing (i.e. an afternoon at the beach). My sister goes on and on about being cold at home and yet she can wander the streets of Croydon on a December night in not much more than a thong.

We have a few false starts but manage to get through 'Born to be Wild' and 'Bed of Razorz' and all finish roughly at the same time.

My sister and Darla clap politely, which isn't really the emotionally charged response we're after but at least they're not chucking bottles of piss. I think Darla may have the hots for Davey. He'd be well in there, as Darla has a job and that brand new limited edition red Mini Cooper. I'm keeping my fingers crossed for him.

"Thank you," says Peter. "And now for our third number, the totally awesome, all-time classic, 'Paranoid' by Black Sabbath!"

"Oh, not *that* old chestnut," moans my sister.

"Eh?" says Peter.

"Can't you do something a bit more original?"

Peter looks at me.

"Just ignore her, Peter," I say.

"Er, hello, we're your audience," says my sister. "Ignore us at your peril!"

"She has a point," says Peter.

I'm getting annoyed so I say, "Look, my sister wouldn't know a good song if it ran up and puked in her hair."

"Fine," says Maddie, getting off the windowsill. "If that's what you think. Come on, Darla."

"No, no," Peter grovels, "please don't go... We still have our big finale, 'The Final Countdown'!"

"Oh God, quick, Darla!" cries my sister.

"Um, OK, well, thanks again for coming tonight," continues Peter as they grab their coats. "We do this for you, our fans. You are what makes it all..."

"Fantastic drumming," Darla says to Davey as she follows my sister out of the room.

"Oh, er, you're welcome," says Davey, beaming.

Friday 24th December – Christmas Eve!

4.45pm: Inner Sanctum, wrapping presents with Ozzy

This is Ozzy's favourite time of year as he can leap about in the wrapping paper, play peek-a-boo, let out small wees and generally make wrapping presents a complete and utter nightmare!

This year, I have been very organised and got all my presents *before* the shops shut. In previous years, I've been too late and had to make gifts out of stuff I found at the back of my wardrobe and under my bed. I once gave Mum the same little grey bear hugging a silver star three years in a row and she didn't even realise!

Ollie texts to say:

Guess what! I got a last-minute cancellation at the test centre and passed!

Surely this has to be a joke. Ollie is a danger to himself and everyone else on the road/pavement.

Another text from Ollie:

Wanna go 2 Cornwall?

Text from me:

Ollie, do not drive to Cornwall, u idiot! U'll get lost/die and we need u in the band. Well done on passing, BTW.

Text from Ollie:

Tesco, then. I need 2 buy a present 4 Rose.

Text from me:

Tesco shut, u r screwed. Ha! Happy xmas 4 tomoz, BTW.

Saturday 25th December – Christmas Day!

8.00am: Lounge, opening presents

I have been up since 6.45am. I don't know why I still get excited about Christmas; however, it looks like this year I've at least got one good present...

"It's a Children of Bodom t-shirt!" I say, almost choking on a mouthful of chocolate brazils.

"Yes!" says my sister. "Put it on."

I pull the t-shirt over my head and look down at my chest. "Hey, it's really cool."

"I know it's not much, but I've got something else for you," says my sister. "Something I think you'll like. I'll try and get it to you over the next couple of days."

"Well, I really like this," I tell her. And it's true, I do.

"Now open one from me," I say, passing over a big, flat parcel.

I have bought my sister several presents this year: earplugs to stop her incessant complaining about my music, a Brad Pitt calendar which features him topless in March, August and November, and a small grey bear holding a star.

My sister takes a glug from her sherry glass before gently removing the wrapping paper. We can't rip it because Mum is watching and it has to be used again next year and the year after, etc.

"Oooh!" she says, her eyes going dreamy. "Let me check the picture for my birthday."

My sister's birthday is on the 10th August.

"Yes!" she cries. "Phwoar! Would you look at those abs!"

Honestly, my sister needs to get a grip on herself. The way she pervs over the male of the species is disgusting. You'd never catch me doing stuff like that with women ;-)

Next, I open a present from Mum.

Cool. It's a new leather-bound notebook; a very classy one with a red padded cover and gold edges to all the pages.

"Look inside," prompts Mum.

Tucked in a paper pocket on the inside cover are two tickets for... Download, the rock festival!

"That's from Ned and me," says Mum.

This is awesome. I mean, *really* awesome. I'm embarrassed to admit it, being such a seasoned and experienced rock fan, but I have never actually been to a festival. At least, not unless you count my middle school's festival of song and interpretive dance, which you definitely shouldn't. Yes! I can't wait for the summer now.

Mum opens the presents I've given her: a handy kitchen caddy for carrying condiments and sauces made out of a cardboard six-pack holder, a flower pot made from a pot noodle container (washed and painted), some chocolate brazils (buy one get one free at Morrisons) and a DVD of her favourite film, *Bridget Jones's*

Diary – although why anyone would be interested in what's in someone else's diary is beyond me.

10.30am

It's still only the morning, but I'm already laid on the sofa in a food/crap TV/booze coma. We have eaten two boxes of chocolate brazils, a tube of Pringles and some Turkish Delight. We have also drunk most of a bottle of sherry and watched the whole of the diary film. But so what? It's Christmas!

Sunday 26th December

3.00pm: Inner Sanctum

I spend all day going over our songs for the New Year's gig. I really hope the others are practising too. After our last session, I told Peter to work on his intro and between-song repartee. I said, "This is metal, Peter. Remember, metal takes no prisoners."

"Right," said Peter.

"You have to give 'em hell."

"Hell. OK, will do."

Why am I not reassured?

10.30pm

I forgot to give the fox any food last night so I give him a big selection tonight. His Christmas present is a day late but as he's unlikely to be religious I'm guessing he won't mind.

He gets:

some sliced chicken

two burnt chipolatas

five Brussels sprouts

three roast potatoes

a small ball of stuffing

a fifth of a treacle pudding with congealed custard

one slightly weird-tasting Brazil nut, part sucked,

      hence minus chocolate.

He is there almost as soon as I get back upstairs, looking up at my window.

Merry Christmas, Mr Fox!

Monday 27th December

3.30pm: Moving all the band stuff to Peter's dad's flat in Ollie's car

"I still think this idea is insane," I tell Peter, as we lug the amps into his dad's flat. Thank God it's a ground-floor one.

"It is," says Peter, "but that's why people will love it!" I'll give Peter his due; he's a real positive thinker.

Ollie has parked directly outside the communal entrance, which will probably get him ticketed, so we try to be quick but there's lots to carry. Luckily, the flat has an enormous lounge. It's like one of those open-plan New York City lofts you see in American films, except rather than having a view of the New York skyline, it has a view of the back of Tesco.

"I thought we could play up here," says Peter, wandering over to the top of the lounge where there are some swanky glass bookcases and cabinets lining the walls. "We'll put the food and booze on tables along the side there. On New Year's Eve we can move some of the furniture into the bedrooms so people have room to dance."

This seems a good plan so we set up the amps, stands and drums, etc. in front of the cabinets.

"Thank your dad for letting us do this," I say to Peter, although 99.9% of me wishes he hadn't.

Peter nods. "He was dead keen. You know what parents are like after a divorce."

I don't really, but I can guess.

We spend a couple of hours practising and it's sounding quite good, but then Lloyd says he has to go to a church thing so we pack up.

"I hope it goes well for your mum tomorrow," says Davey, as he shrugs on his coat.

"Yeah," says Ollie, giving me a fist bump.

Then Peter suddenly grabs me in a bear hug – luckily a very brief one – and says, "Don't worry. Your mum is indestructible."

"Yeah, I know," I tell them, laughing. "She's like a cockroach!"

6.00pm: Some streets

Heading home a few minutes later, I am wondering about what Peter said. Until recently, Mum really did seem indestructible. She was always so in control. Nothing could stop her... or almost nothing. I think about her marching my mates and me back through the park last summer when we'd all had too much to drink. It wasn't funny then, but it makes me smile now.

It should be rush hour but it's strangely quiet on the streets. I plunge my hands deep in my pockets and walk home fast. The wind is making my eyes water and there are a few flakes of snow in it.

Tuesday 28th December

5.05pm: Hospital with sister and Mum

We are in **the** Augustine ward saying our goodbyes to Mum.

"See you tomorrow," she says cheerfully. "And stay off the chocolates!"

"We will," we promise.

We pause at the ward exit and wave goodbye.

Mum waves back.

Before we left home, Maddie told me she was worried she might cry but she has kept it together really well... at least until we get inside the lift.

"Good thing Mum didn't tell us to stay off the sherry," she says once the lift doors have closed. "Darla and me finished that second bottle last night and I don't even like sherry!"

"Ha!" I say, and when I look over I see that she is laughing and crying at the same time.

Wednesday 29th December

9.30am: Inner Sanctum

If things are running to plan, then Mum should be going into surgery now. I don't know how to pray or even if it works but I just say "Please God, let Mum be OK" in my head.

11.30am: Peter's Inner Sanctum

We are in crisis talks regarding the party. Peter is worried about the food. "Are ten pizzas enough?" he asks.

"It depends how many are coming," says Ollie.

"I *don't know* how many are coming," whines Peter. "That's the problem. And even if I *did*, I don't know what sort of pizza they'd like. Do they want deep pan or crispy? Crusts stuffed or plain? Are they vegetarian? Do they have allergies? Oh my God! It's out of control!"

"Peter," says Davey, "Calm down. You don't want to have a party-planning panic attack."

Peter drops his head in his hands.

"Breathe slowly, Peter," Davey tells him. "Count to three, then exhale."

Peter inhales and exhales deeply for a while before opening his eyes and looking up. "OK," he says. "I can do this. I'll order ten large pizzas, four vegetarian, three meat supreme, three tuna melt. I'll get six bags of tortilla chips, two cool chilli, three ready salted, one pesto and sun-dried peppers, plus four bags of kettle chips – various varieties. I will buy three twelve-packs of beer, two litres of diet lemonade and two litres of diet Coke. What with people bringing their own booze, I think that should be enough. Yes?"

I nod, but to be honest, I think the food is the least of our worries.

5.00pm: Hospital, visiting Mum after her operation

"Oh God," my sister says, as we make our way to Mum's ward, our shoes squeaking on the polished floors. "I really do *hate* hospitals. Why do they make them so serious and clinical-looking?"

Er, because they're hospitals?

"I don't know," I say. "They do have some nice murals on the walls."

"That doesn't fool anybody," snaps my sister.

To be honest, I hate hospitals too. Not just because there are people who are ill or injured, although that's part of it. It's also because I'm worried I'll do something really stupid, like knock over a trolley full of life-saving instruments or have a fit of wildly inappropriate laughter. Maybe I'm worried they're gonna think I'm mad and section me.

Anyway, we find Mum at the far end of a ward of six people, all of whom seem pretty miserable. Mum looks tired and is bandaged up but she manages to raise a smile and gestures for us to come and sit down. Maddie takes the vinyl chair and I settle on the end of the bed. I have only just sat down, however, when I am shouted at by a nurse.

"No sitting on beds!" she snaps.

I apologise and pull a chair up from the cubicle of the lady-next-door. She's asleep, so I guess she won't mind.

"Well, this is nice!" exclaims my sister, looking around the bleakly clinical ward and smiling as if we're in the penthouse suite of some five-star hotel.

"Yes," says Mum. "And everyone's been so helpful. What have you two been getting up to?"

"Josh has been practising the guitar," says Maddie. "And I've been cleaning."

"I did some cleaning too!" I say.

"Not as much as me."

This is a total lie, but it's probably not a good time to get into a major argument.

We don't stay long because the scary nurse tells us we are making Mum tired, and we should come back tomorrow.

I am starting to hate hospitals even more but Mum manages to give me a wink as we go, so I feel a bit better.

Thursday 30th December

3.30pm: Peter's dad's place

Bad news. We have practised so much that Lloyd's fingers are bleeding! Also, Davey has repetitive strain injury, Peter's voice has gone super-squeaky, and stress has turned my face into an acne-ridden minefield. We have to give it a rest or we won't be able to even go to the party tomorrow, let alone play at it.

5.30pm: Hospital, seeing Mum

We are getting used to the hospital now and can find the ward really easily. I drag the chair up from the lady next door, who is still sleeping (at least I hope that's what she's doing), and my sister sits in her usual seat. I look around for the Nazi nurse but luckily she doesn't appear to be on duty today.

"How are you feeling?" asks my sister.

"Oh, OK," I say.

"Not you, you idiot!"

Mum laughs, but I think it hurts a bit when she does as I see her wince.

We stay for about thirty minutes tonight, which is pretty good. I think Mum is getting better and I think my sister agrees. She doesn't say much but she is humming 'Stronger' by Kelly Clarkson as we get in the lift.

Friday 31st December – New Year's Eve

11.20am: Hallway

I've just got back from getting a few bits of essential shopping down the Co-op (chocolate and crisps) when my sister starts grinning like a hyena that's won the national lottery for hyenas. She grabs me by both shoulders, swivels me round and says: "The second part of your Christmas present is in the lounge. Go on in."

I wander into the lounge and am suddenly confronted by a heavily tattooed, six ft four giant with a ginger beard/hair combo.

Luckily, I manage to steady myself against the sofa or I think I may have collapsed with shock.

"Um, hello," I manage.

"Aye," grunts the giant.

"It's not a weird Scottish strippergram, is it?" I whisper to Maddie, who has come to stand beside me.

"No, you fool!" she cries. "This is Angus. He's come to do your tattoo!"

8.00pm: Peter's New Year's Eve party!

Peter's party is starting to warm up. Beyoncé is on the stereo (metaphorically, she'd probably break it if she was actually stood on it) and there are about a dozen people, all hipsters, laughing and helping themselves to drinks.

"Who *are* they?" I ask Peter.

Peter grins, a little manically. "I have absolutely no idea!"

"This is Rose," says Ollie, coming over.

"Oh, hi Rose," I say. "Finally, we get to meet. I was starting to think Ollie had made you up!"

"Er, nope," says Rose, grinning and putting her hands on her hips. "I'm pretty much for real."

Rose has red hair like Angus the tattooist. Whenever I see a red-haired person I'm reminded of a ginger cat. I'm not being mean saying that. Ginger cats are not unattractive. Possibly not as pleasing on the eye as, say, a silver tabby or Bengal but... Wait a minute, this is starting to sound like I fancy cats, which I definitely don't! Anyway, Rose says, "I hear you have a new tattoo."

"Oh yes," says Davey. "Can we see it in the flesh? Oh, pun!"

I carefully lift up the sleeve of my t-shirt and gently peel away the cellophane that's covering the tattoo. The skin's a bit red and I've had to smear on some special greasy stuff to stop it drying out, but you can still see it pretty well.

"Wow!" says Peter. "That's great."

"Thanks," I say. "It took a long time."

"It's totally, amazingly cool," says Rose, who I've decided I like. "I have a tattoo of a Labrador on my arse."

"Mutt on a butt!" exclaims Davey. "Can we see..."

"No!" snaps Ollie.

Lloyd appears with a huge slice of pizza and what is probably his sixth beer of the evening. "All right?" he says.

I nod but the truth is my digestive system is shot to pieces due to nerves.*

And I daren't drink or I won't be able to perform my incredibly fast and technically challenging solos. This is the trouble with being the musical wizard in the band: you can't chill out at all.

Just then, Davey's phone launches into the theme tune from *The Great British Bake-Off*, which means he's got a text. "It's from Darla," he says, "wishing us luck."

We're gonna need it.

11.30pm: Goat Fiend's first-ever gig!

OK, this is it. We are pumped, psyched and ready to go. Ollie takes his place by the keyboards and I see him crack his knuckles a few times. Davey sits at his drums and does his stretches. Lloyd and me manage to put our guitars on the right way round and Peter saunters up slowly to his mic, trying and failing to look cool. I'm really hoping he can see what he's doing because in those shades it must be pitch black in here. Anyway, he grabs the mic and surprises everyone (including me) by suddenly yelling, "**YEAAAAAH!**" really loud.

Then he says, "OK, are you ready to rock?"

A few of the crowd say, "Sure. Aha. I guess," that sort of thing, but most are still in shock from the initial YEAAAH. So Peter snatches the mic stand forcibly and screams, "I said, are you ready to rock, MOTHERF***ERS?"

Jesus. Good job his dad isn't here.

"YEAH!" the crowd yells back.

Peter nods. "All right! We are Goat Fiend and we are gonna BLOW. YOUR. MIND!"

* *I had to use virtually a whole can of Glade in Peter's dad's toilet.*

Davey counts us in and starts the song, Ollie comes in right on cue and then it's me. Yes, nailed it! Before I can relax, though, I'm on to the solo. This is where all those hours of practice start to pay off (hopefully). I look up to see people playing air guitar and head-banging. Are they taking the piss? I don't know, but whatever they're doing they seem to be enjoying it.

We finish the song exactly together. Wow, somebody pinch me! Everyone claps and we get a few whistles of encouragement. I can't believe how well this is going.

"Thank you, A**HOLES!" cries Peter.

Before they can get bored we launch into 'Born to be Wild' and then straight into 'Paranoid'. Davey's tricky drum solo is coming up and out of my peripheral vision, I see a drumstick go flying in the air. It twirls around several times before being expertly caught. How did he do that? How? Davey performs his solos without missing a beat. If I hadn't been here I wouldn't have believed it. In fact, I don't believe it. He looks the spitting image of Dave Lombardo (Slayer/Testament).

We get to the end and the applause is deafening. Much of it, I suspect, is for Davey who, shaking his hair free of sweat, stands up and bows.

"And now for our final number," says Peter.

"Nooo!" shouts the audience.

It's 11.50pm and we are about to launch into 'The Final Countdown'. The idea is to finish a few minutes before midnight to give us a chance to raise our glasses and let Peter lead a musically accompanied countdown to the New Year. If it works, it will actually be pretty epic.

Davey nods, takes up his sticks and commences to count

us in, but before the sticks can make contact Davey suddenly disappears and there is an ENORMOUS crash!

I watch, speechless, as all hell is let loose. Cymbals, drums and sticks fly everywhere. Glass shatters and the bookcases behind us lean forward, showering Ollie with paperbacks and various china ornaments. Peter tries to move out of the way but gets his legs caught round the mic cable and falls flat on his face in a tortured wail of feedback. For a few seconds, I am not sure where I am or even if I'm still alive. It's like we've been hit by a tornado...

11.56pm: Five minutes later

Ah God, somehow we have got to our feet and managed to right the bookcases and find our disappearing drummer. Davey had fallen back into the glass bookshelves, causing them to topple. He had tried to sit on a chair that was no longer there, a chair that he'd knocked over after standing up for applause. He is now groaning and complaining of a headache and a busted arse.

Meanwhile, Ollie is staggering around in a daze after being hit by a low-flying china swan. He has a nasty gash on his forehead that will probably need stitches. Peter is appealing for calm but his shades are bent at a ridiculous angle and his leather trousers have ripped up the back to show his Spongebob SquarePants boxers. He looks like he's been pushed through a food blender backwards. Meanwhile, Lloyd is throwing up in a plant pot. And the crowd...? Well, the crowd are loving every minute!

"Quick, everyone," says Peter, spying the clock. "It's nearly time for the dongs! I mean it's nearly time for the F****ING

DONGS! Everyone, grab a drink."

We can't do our musical thing now, so Peter puts on the TV just as the countdown comes on. He joins in with Jools Holland, still full of enthusiasm (Peter, not Jools), despite the carnage around us.

"Ten" he cries.

"Nine!

Eight!

Six!

Oh sorry, seven!

Um, three...

Two...

One!!!!

Happy New Year, everyone!"

Saturday 1st January

2.00pm: Augustine Ward, hospital

Mum is much brighter today. She is sitting up in bed and smiling. The nurses say she can come home tomorrow.

"Did you have a good New Year's Eve?" she asks me. "What did you get up to?"

"Oh, not much," I say. "It was quiet, you know."

My sister quickly goes to look out the window, but I can hear her barely stifled sniggering from here. She knows all about last night. Kudos to her, though, since despite a hard night's flirting at Tiger Tiger she and Darla came round to Peter's dad's at about 3am and helped us to clean up.

Darla and Davey left together, soon after 5am. Davey was

still complaining about his arse and Darla offered to soothe it using the healing powers of massage in the back of her red Mini Cooper!

Oh well, it's now or never, I guess. "Er, Mum," I say. "I got a tattoo."

"A tattoo!" exclaims Mum, struggling to sit upright.

"Please don't be mad," I say. "I can easily hide it when I go for interviews. I've wanted one for ages and I promise I won't get any more. Not if you don't want me to."

Mum sighs and says, "I suppose it's some hideous skull or scythe or something."

I look at my sister and grimace.

"Oh well, let's see it then," says Mum.

I take off my jacket, lift up my sleeve and show her my arm.

"What do you think?" I ask.

Mum shakes her head and gives me a little smile. "I think it's really nice," she says.

11.45pm: Inner Sanctum

I turn to the list in my leather-bound notebook and put a tick beside *Get a tattoo*. Sorted!

It's 1st January, so I guess I ought to make a new list – a list of New Year's resolutions. I could even use my book with the red padded cover and gold edges!

"What should they be, then?" I ask Ozzy, opening it carefully.

Ozzy bounds over and starts rolling about on the pages. He doesn't believe in making lists. He doesn't worry about New Year's resolutions, being popular, looking good and all that stuff. Maybe that's because he has a strong sense of self, a knowledge of what's truly important and an unshakable inner peace.

Or maybe it's because he's a ferret.

ABOUT THE AUTHOR

J. A. Buckle studied Zoology at university, and now works for the national drug charity DrugScope. She is also the author of *Half My Facebook Friends Are Ferrets*. As well as writing, she designs websites, helps out at animal welfare charities and an eating disorder charity, plays guitar and takes her dog for walks. She has two teenage children and lives in Surrey.

NEED HELP?

Do you or someone you know experience panic attacks or anxiety?

Panic attacks and anxiety are a very upsetting problem for many people. According to the charity Anxiety UK, as many as one in six young people will experience an anxiety problem at some point in their lives. So, if you do suffer from anxiety it's important to remember that you are not alone and support is available. You may find it helpful to look at the YOUNG MINDS website (www.youngminds.org.uk) which has lots of information on anxiety and panic attacks, including possible causes and how you can access treatment and support. It also includes tips for helping yourself, and guidance for friends and family.

If you have a parent or close relative suffering from cancer, you may find these websites helpful:

Macmillan – **www.macmillan.org.uk/Cancerinformation/If-someoneelsehascancer/Youngcarers/Youngcarers.aspx**

RipRap – **www.riprap.org.uk**

More titles from Curious Fox

Half My Facebook Friends are Ferrets

Josh Walker – AKA Josh the Destroyer – has rock 'n' roll dreams, but his mum won't even let him grow his hair long. His best friends are either geeks or nerds (they haven't decided yet) and he's had precisely zero Valentine's Day cards in his life. Will he ever live up to the cool, tough dad he's never known?

The Soterion Mission

In a post-apocalyptic world where no-one lives beyond their teenage years, the mysterious Roxanne arrives in Cyrus's village, fleeing the barbaric Zeds. She claims to be on a mission that can save them all, but can she be trusted? Cyrus joins her in her quest for the legendary Soterion, but the Zeds are determined to get there first.

"...one of those thought-provoking novels... the way in which Ross left certain sections with cliffhangers just helped me keep turning the pages in anticipation."
Callie Reads on *The Soterion Mission*

"If you are looking for a rip-roaring read that gets you thinking, then pick up Revenge of the Zeds."
Of Life and Literature on *Revenge of the Zeds*

For more exciting books from
brilliant authors, follow the fox!

www.curious-fox.com